A Sy

Welcome

Harper, Ivy, Al ... ne
top at Sydney Central. Along the way, they've weathered the highs and lows of life but one thing has always remained steadfast: their friendship!

Now life's about to take an unexpected turn for the friends—it seems that Cupid has checked into Sydney Central Hospital!

Come and experience the rush of falling in love as these four feisty heroines meet their matches…

Harper and the Single Dad by Amy Andrews
Ivy's Fling with the Surgeon by Louisa George

Available now!

Ali and the Rebel Doc by Emily Forbes
Phoebe's Baby Bombshell by JC Harroway

Coming July 2023!

Dear Reader,

Thank you for picking up *Ivy's Fling with the Surgeon*. When my editor asked me to be involved in a four-book project with some fabulous Harlequin Medical Romance authors (Amy Andrews, JC Harroway and Emily Forbes), I jumped at the chance! It is always wonderful to immerse yourself in a glamorous setting like Sydney and I loved creating the characters, hospital, roof gardens and local café with the author team.

Ivy and Lucas both adore Sydney too, and I had a lot of fun having them explore the city and environs together while trying to fight an increasingly sizzling attraction. The plan is to get to know each other enough to fool Lucas's parents into thinking they're in a relationship. Not to actually be in one…right? Neither of them are in it for the long haul but the longer they're together, the deeper they fall…

I hope you love Lucas and Ivy's story as much as I enjoyed writing it.

I love to hear from readers, so please feel free to get in touch via my website, www.louisageorge.com.

Happy reading!

Louisa xx

IVY'S FLING WITH THE SURGEON

LOUISA GEORGE

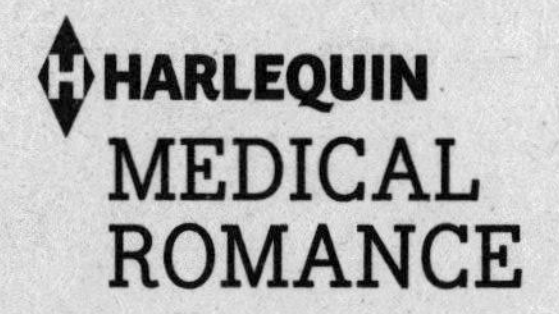

Special thanks and acknowledgment are given to Louisa George for her contribution to the A Sydney Central Reunion miniseries.

Recycling programs for this product may not exist in your area.

ISBN-13: 978-1-335-73793-9

Ivy's Fling with the Surgeon

For questions and comments about the quality of this book, please contact us at CustomerService@Harlequin.com.

Harlequin Enterprises ULC
22 Adelaide St. West, 41st Floor
Toronto, Ontario M5H 4E3, Canada
www.Harlequin.com

Printed in U.S.A.

Award-winning author **Louisa George** has been an avid reader her whole life. In between chapters, she's managed to train as a nurse, marry her doctor hero and have two sons. Now she writes chapters of her own in the medical romance, contemporary romance and women's fiction genres. Louisa's books have variously been nominated for the coveted RITA® Award and the New Zealand Koru Award, and have been translated into twelve languages. She lives in Auckland, New Zealand.

Books by Louisa George

Harlequin Medical Romance

Rawhiti Island Medics

Resisting the Single Dad Next Door

Royal Christmas at Seattle General

The Princess's Christmas Baby

SOS Docs

Saved by Their One-Night Baby

Reunited by Their Secret Son
A Nurse to Heal His Heart
A Puppy and a Christmas Proposal
Nurse's One-Night Baby Surprise
ER Doc to Mistletoe Bride
Cornish Reunion with the Heart Doctor

Visit the Author Profile page at Harlequin.com for more titles.

Writing is always better when you're part of a team. So thank you to Amy Andrews, Emily Forbes and JC Harroway for making this project such fun!

Praise for
Louisa George

"A single dad, an unexpected pregnancy, secret crush, friends to lovers, Louisa George combines so many of my favourite tropes in her latest outing to Oakdale… This series is right up there with Sarah Morgan's medical romances…and it's no secret how much I love those."

—*Goodreads* on *Nurse's One-Night Baby Surprise*

CHAPTER ONE

PAPERWORK WAS INVENTED by someone with a sick sense of humour. Probably a man.

Dr Ivy Hurst stared at the hundreds of messages, results and requests in her work inbox and sighed.

Once upon a time I had a life other than this.

But at least paperwork didn't cheat on you.

Her phone vibrated on her desk and the upbeat ringtone she used for her three best friends, Phoebe, Harper and Alinta, blared into the otherwise silent room. She glanced at the caller ID. Phoebe.

Smiling, she clicked onto speakerphone so she could chat and work at the same time. 'Hey, Phoebs, how's things?'

'Great.' A pause. 'Ivy Hurst, do I hear keyboard tapping? Please tell me you're not still at work. I left hours ago.'

Busted.

Ivy froze, her fingers hovering in mid-air as she glanced at the clock on the wall of her messy hospital office. Almost eight-thirty. 'Wow, it's late. How did that happen? I'm just catching up on paperwork. What's up?'

'Thought I'd share Harper's good news: Yarran's finally been discharged.'

Thank goodness.

Ivy breathed out slowly. They'd all been hoping and praying their friend Yarran—Alinta's twin brother—would pull through after a terrible firefighting accident. And here he was, healing and moving on with Harper.

'That is good news. So, they're actually living together now? All going well?' Ivy tried typing quietly so Phoebe wouldn't hear, but then gave up and focused on the conversation. 'I really need to check in with them, but I'm snowed under right now.'

'It's okay, we all understand what it's like to be a doctor, hon. And yes, they're very happy. Talk about loved up, the air almost crackles around them.' Phoebe chuckled, although Ivy imagined her friend also jokingly rolling her eyes. Out of the four of them Harper appeared to be the only one lucky in love, and that had happened only recently.

Ivy sighed. 'I'm so pleased for them. It's taken them a long time to get to this point.'

Harper and Yarran's relationship had been all on years ago, before Harper had gone to London for a job opportunity she just couldn't miss...

breaking Yarran's heart in the process. But now she was back in Sydney and the sparks between Harper and Yarran had been rekindled. Ivy was delighted, but also aware of a pang of envy in her chest, because once upon a time she'd also believed in happily ever after.

'Yes. About twelve years, give or take,' her friend confirmed.

A lot longer than Ivy's last and failed relationship. 'Don't know if I could adjust to living with someone again these days. I don't think I'd be good at sharing my space.'

'You had Harper living with you,' Phoebe quipped back.

'Only until her apartment was ready. We both knew it was only temporary. I mean, sure I loved having her stay with me, she's so easy to have around. She does girl things, she's funny and kind, we're on the same wavelength. A guy…' Ivy shuddered, remembering how she'd had to tiptoe around her ex when he'd had a bad day. And, towards the end when he didn't come home the odd night and was cryptic about his plans, how she had her suspicions about where he was and with who. 'It's complicated navigating all that, right?'

Phoebe tsked. 'That's because you're too nice. You need to put yourself and your needs on an equal footing with everyone else.'

'Ha. I did that with my parents, and it didn't

go down at all well. It's taken them years to forgive me. I'm not really sure they have.'

'If you'd gone into the army like they wanted you'd never have met us at medical school. Imagine a life without me, Alinta and Harper.'

'No, thanks. I don't want to think about that ever happening.' When Harper had left, Alinta had been almost as devastated as her brother and things between Harper and Alinta had become very strained. But now everything was settling down again and the four friends were back living in the same city. 'It's even better now we're all working at the Central too.'

'And Yarran just down the road at the fire station.'

'It's perfect. Well, almost. Unfortunately, Grant's still here.' Ivy shuddered again.

Phoebe's tone became all businesslike. 'With a bit of luck your no-good ex will find a job somewhere else. I'll keep an eye out on the job listings and forward him the ones the furthest away. I'm sure they need more urologists in Outer Mongolia. Anyway, Yarran is nothing like Grant.'

'True.' Ivy laughed. 'Harper wouldn't take any nonsense anyway. At least, not twice, like I did.'

'You're too forgiving, Ivy.'

'I did not forgive his cheating.'

'You gave him a second chance.'

I gave him a lot more than that. My heart. My trust. Which he stomped all over.

'He said it was a blip and the affair meant nothing to him. That he loved me, and I was his life.' She put her head in her hands and laughed wryly. 'Until the next pretty woman came along. Men, huh? I'm way too old for all that game-playing.'

Phoebe snorted. 'You're not even forty. Unlike the rest of us.'

'Not far off. I'm staring it down. And, you know, I thought I'd be…well, *not single* at this ripe old age.'

'Hey, steady on with the old. It's not so bad. Honestly. Actually, it's fun.'

'If you keep men out of the equation.' Ivy knew Phoebe was also determinedly single.

But to her surprise Phoebe laughed. 'There are some good ones out there. Case in point: Yarran.'

'True. He's a keeper. But, to be honest, it's so much easier being single. No navigating emotional minefields, no second-guessing myself, and definitely no gaslighting. Men are strictly off limits from now on. Especially charming, good-looking ones.'

'Ahem.'

Oops.

The very masculine sound had Ivy whirling round in her swivel chair to find Lucas Matthews, Head of Reconstructive Surgery, leaning casually against her door frame. With his expensive-looking navy-blue suit, crisp white shirt and perfectly tousled dark hair, he wore the arrogant air of someone who knew he was good-looking and had a reputation almost as bad as her ex's. Apparently, he'd left a trail of broken hearts across the previous hospital he'd worked in and was making inroads into the single female staff population here at Sydney Central.

Good-looking: yes. Charming: big fat no.

At least she wouldn't be tempted by the likes of him.

She blinked as she regarded him. He had a sort of amused smile, which gave her the distinct impression he'd heard—or had been listening to—her conversation. Heat hit her cheeks. Which, at the ripe age of thirty-nine, was something she really wished she had a handle on by now.

'Listen, Phoebs, got to go.' She grabbed her phone, jabbing at the buttons to cut the call before her friend could say anything more incriminating. Worse, Lucas Matthews now knew about her sad love life, which she generally chose to keep private given her ex was still employed at the Central too.

He straightened up. 'Sorry to interrupt your obviously *very important* conversation, Dr Hurst.' His tone was as sharp as his fancy jacket lapel points and, while their paths had crossed on more than a few occasions, they were very definitely not on first-name terms. 'But we need to talk.'

'We do?' What could they possibly need to talk about at this time of night?

And how dare he listen in on a private conversation and then judge it?

He stepped into the room, filling her space with his overbearing presence. 'About Emma Wilson. I've just been reviewing her up on the ward and hear you've been called in to assess her.'

Ah. Their shared patient: a twenty-six-year-old woman with bad burns to her lower legs following a house fire. Ivy wasn't sure what hackles were, but she felt hers immediately jump to attention. This wasn't the first time they'd discussed appropriate treatment plans and timelines for shared patients, and it probably wasn't going to be the last. He wanted to dive in early, Ivy wanted to make sure Emma was physically able to deal with any further intervention.

'And…?' she invited him to elucidate.

'I want to operate. Tomorrow.'

'Whoa. No way. Not so fast. I've only just been to see her.' Ivy held up her palm. 'I need to get to the bottom of her spiking temperatures and abdo pain before she has any more interventions.'

'And I need to operate.'

'I may need to, too.' She huffed. 'But I'm trying to avoid it if I can. She's twenty-eight weeks pregnant with twins and only recently been brought out of an induced coma. She has a lot going on and it's all a big draw on what little resources she has left. Surely plastic surgery can wait just a little bit longer until she's stable.'

His eyes widened in what she took as irritation. Possibly anger. 'It's not as if this is a vanity project, Dr Hurst. Firstly, I need to debride some of her grafts because the infection risk is real. And secondly, post-burn hypertrophic scars are thick, and painful. This poor woman, who, as you say, has been through a lot already, is at risk of developing contractions that could lead to limited movement, even deformity. If we're going to minimise long-term pain and scarring, time is of the essence.'

He had a point and, more, he seemed highly invested in Emma's care. Clearly, she wasn't the only doctor protective of her patients. She breathed out slowly in an effort to control her irritation. Why did she feel so combative around this man? There was something about him that rubbed her up the wrong way.

'If we can get on top of this current crisis then you can start the reconstruction surgery but I'm in no position to give you a timeline. The abdominal pain doesn't appear to be related to her pregnancy or accident, as far as we can tell. We're waiting on scans, swabs and white cell count. As soon as we get those we can target with the right treatment and appropriate antibiotics.'

'Thanks. I am aware of how to treat an infection, Dr Hurst.' His intense brown eyes bored into her. There was a thick, almost tangible, energy in the air.

But she refused to back down or look away. 'Good. Then you'll understand my reluctance to allow any further infection risk. My registrar is looking after Emma tonight and will keep me informed of any changes. So, I'll let you know as soon as I know.'

She turned back to face her monitor. Hopefully he'd get the hint and leave.

But his voice deepened. 'Make it quick.'

'Excuse me?' As she whirled back to look at him Ivy Hurst's dark eyes glittered with ill-concealed anger, her body tight and stiff. She jumped up, pushing back her office chair so brusquely she sent it barrelling towards him. '*What* did you say?'

Lucas cringed. As soon as the words had escaped his mouth he regretted them, but he'd been unable to stop them. There was something about her that brought out a niggly irritation in him. Who did she think she was to dictate when he should do his job?

Her caller had said she was too nice? Too forgiving? Ha! Not something he'd witnessed so far.

'I said...it needs to be quick.' He caught the chair as it slowed in front of him.

Her gaze drifted from him to the chair and

back in mild interest. Then anything mild deserted her gaze the second she refocused on his face. 'Dr Matthews, I appreciate the concern for your patient, but this is not the army…' Her nostrils flared at that, then she added, 'I do not take orders from anyone. And particularly not when it comes to the welfare of my patient.'

Great.

He huffed out a breath. Today had been hard enough without this spat. He'd lost a patient in the operating theatre and had another run-in with his parents over the guest list for their charity fundraiser. Was he bringing a plus one? Another veiled attempt at finding out whether he was settling down, and no doubt another opportunity to parade what they believed to be suitable eligible women in front of him, hoping he'd pick one and settle down.

No, thanks.

Plus, he'd missed a call from his younger sister, Flora. As always, the familiar guilt yawned inside him. He worked too many hours, stayed away from the family home too much for him to give her the attention she so deserved.

Now this. He closed his eyes and dredged up some calm. When he opened them again Dr Hurst was still staring at him as if he were the devil incarnate. He raised his hand to try to mollify her. 'It wasn't an order. Just a request. Look, we both want what's best for Emma. We're on the same page.'

'Oh, trust me, we're not even in the same book.' She shoved a hand through her caramel-coloured bobbed hair and glared at him, her brown eyes glittering and sparking. This close he could see flashes of green and gold in her irises. An angry mouth. One triangle of her white cotton blouse hem had untucked from her short khaki linen skirt, which looked as if it had never seen an iron. She was ruffled in more ways than one.

She was petite and had to tilt her head to look up at him, but she had a distinct aura of authority. Given her seniority, she was probably around his age, and he knew how hard it was to work your way up the medical career ladder—she'd probably had to fight to get to the top. She wouldn't take fools gladly and right now she was standing her ground.

Too forgiving, my arse.

Talking of… He glanced down…yes, he hadn't noticed before—in truth, he'd never looked—but she had curves in all the right places. A formidable woman, passionate and fiery.

He stepped back. Because those kinds of thoughts about a colleague were inappropriate. 'I'd like to think we could at least have a civil conversation.'

An eyebrow rose. 'Why?'

'So we can work together on the best outcomes for Emma. Surely it doesn't have to be this difficult. I'm not averse to compromise, as long as it doesn't negatively impact my patients.'

She looked away. Swallowed. Then turned back to him. 'I am working with you. Trying to get her well enough for your surgery. This is *all* about Emma.' She glanced down at the chair again. 'You don't need to barricade yourself in. I don't bite.'

Oh, but she wanted to.

He held in a laugh. 'I was trying to stop it from taking out both my legs.'

'Hey!' A frail man in a billowing hospital gown and wheeling an IV stand appeared at the door, one hand on the stand, the other a tight fist, which he thrust towards Dr Hurst. 'Get out. Get out of here.'

Her eyes grew wide. 'Mr Templeton? What on earth are you doing here…?'

The old man frowned, clearly confused and scared. His voice was wobbly and weak but laced with a thinly veiled threat. 'Why are you in my house? You'd better get the hell off my property before I call the police.'

'Mervyn, you're in hospital. You're recovering from an operation to your gallbladder. Look, we need to get you back to the ward. You need to rest and heal.' Clearly snapping straight into assessment mode, Dr Hurst started to walk towards the man with both her palms up in a gesture of conciliation, but not before she threw a quick look towards Lucas that said, *Join the hell in, why don't you?*

But he hadn't liked the man's deathly pallor, the shaking hands, and disorientation, so was already jabbing his phone. 'Can we have a porter to the third-floor admin suite? Now, please? Wheelchair if that's all you've got, but preferably a trolley. Now.'

'And who the hell left all the lights on in the middle of the nigh…? Ugh…' The man crumpled against the IV stand, gripping it, then tipping it as he fell to the floor. His IV line ripped from his arm, the stand crashing as it landed.

Lucas ran to him, joining Dr Hurst on the floor at Mervyn's side. She pressed her fingers against his carotid feeling for a pulse. 'Well, he's still alive. But damn. What the hell…? I only operated on him yesterday—he shouldn't be down here.'

'He's obviously confused, he must have wandered off the ward.' Lucas pressed his fingers against the man's IV site to stop the bleeding. 'Don't suppose there's any sterile packs in your office? I'll get this set up again in the other arm.'

'No packs. But hit the crash button. Behind my desk.'

He dashed back into her office, hit the button and returned with her stethoscope and a digital blood-pressure machine he'd found on her desk. He wrapped the cuff around Mervyn's thin arm.

'Mervyn! Oh, Merv. Please help him.' A frail voice came from behind them, followed by the sound of uncertain, halting steps.

'Mrs Templeton, it's not a good idea for you to be here seeing this.' Dr Hurst looked over at the elderly lady walking towards them. 'He's had a fall; we're just sorting him out.'

But the woman bent down and shook her husband's shoulder. 'Merv. Come on, get up.' She glared at Dr Hurst. 'What's wrong with him? You said you'd fixed his tummy.'

Dr Hurst glanced at the lady and gave her a half-smile that exuded professionalism and compassion and not the slightest bit of irritation, which she must have been feeling because, by unwittingly interrupting, this old lady was well and truly preventing her husband from getting the best possible attention.

But Dr Hurst's voice was soft and concerned… a million miles away from the way she'd spoken to Lucas. 'Please, Mrs Templeton, take a step back. I'm trying to find out what's going on.'

'Hypotensive and tachycardic.' Lucas chose to speak in medical jargon so as not to alert Mrs Templeton to the urgency of the situation. There was more going on here than a post-op faint.

A porter arrived with a stretcher then the crash team appeared, running down the corridor with the crash trolley. Mrs Templeton looked at them all and started to cry. 'What's going on?'

Dr Hurst stood and wrapped an arm around the older lady's shoulder. 'Mervyn's had a faint and we're trying to work out why. Is there anyone we can call to come and sit with you?'

Mrs Templeton worried the hem of her blouse. 'No. Just me and Merv. What can I do?'

'Let us do our job.' Lucas helped attach ECG sticky pads to Mervyn's chest and read the heart trace while Dr Hurst attached another bag of fluids to an IV she'd inserted in his inner elbow, saying, 'I need to take him to Theatre and see what's going on. It's got to be something to do with the surgery.'

'Don't let him die.' Mrs Templeton grabbed Dr Hurst's arm. 'You can't let him die.'

'Mrs Templeton, please let go of the doctor. We need to get him back to Theatre. That's the only way we can save him right now. Come with me. Let's go somewhere you can sit down. Maybe a cup of tea?' Lucas gently peeled the woman's fingers from the trolley, then caught Dr Hurst's eye. As she mouthed the words *thank you* he saw gratitude soften her features. The faintest glimmer of a smile.

Or he might have been imagining it.

Either way he felt an easing of the tension between them.

For now, anyway. Because he was going to

operate on Emma at the earliest opportunity whether Dr Hurst wanted him to or not.

He put his palm on Mrs Templeton's shoulder and coaxed her away so the team could rush their patient towards the lift, but the old lady took a couple of faltering steps forward. 'Mervyn. Please—'

Lucas walked slowly away from the stretcher gently bringing Mrs Wilson with him. 'Dr Hurst will do everything she can to save him. I know she's an excellent doctor.'

If the way she protected Emma was anything to go by she was thorough, dedicated, determined. Stubborn almost. And damned pretty when she smiled. Very pretty actually. Which shouldn't have registered at all, but his skin prickled with something a lot like attraction.

Oh, no.

No way.

He closed his eyes briefly and the image of the corners of her mouth turning up because of something he'd said floated in front of his vision. The light in her eyes. The glint of grit and compassion. A heady mix. An alluring mix.

Just no. He was not going to be attracted to a firecracker like Ivy Hurst. Not when he was going to have to work with her.

That would only make his life a whole lot more difficult.

CHAPTER TWO

Ivy stepped out of the theatre suite, exhaustion nipping at her bones. Thankfully, the unexpected surgery had gone well, and Mr Templeton was safe in Recovery. Now she could go home and get some much-needed sleep.

But she stopped short as she caught sight of Lucas Matthews sitting on a white plastic chair, looking at his phone, only metres from her.

Was he here for her? *No.* No, why would he be waiting for her?

But that thought slid into her belly and made it jitter with something she was annoyed to realise was excitement.

No.

She could not be excited at seeing this man. He was an annoyance. Even if he was a good-looking charmer of an annoyance.

He looked up, stood and put his phone away. She couldn't quite read his expression but if she were to guess it would be concerned. 'Dr Hurst? Hey.'

He *was* waiting for her. Wow. She didn't like the way her skin prickled with excitement and her heart did a little dance at that thought, so she ignored her treacherous body. What was wrong with her today? Why was her body reacting to him like this? 'Dr Matthews?'

And was that her voice? All scratchy and hoarse and come-on sexy?

'Lucas, please.'

Lucas would make him human, and she didn't want that. It was far better to haul emotional barriers up around her. She changed her tone to one of indifference. 'Dr Matthews, what are you doing here?'

His mouth twitched at the corners as he registered her formality. 'I was concerned.'

'About me?'

His throat made a funny—possibly sarcastic—sound. 'About Mr Templeton. I told his wife I'd let her know how he's doing as soon as you came out of Theatre.'

Ah. Stupid treacherous body. 'Informing relatives about the status of *my* patients is my job.'

'I know. But she made me promise and I'm a man of my word.' He gave her a *what can you do?* kind of shrug.

'Oh, yes. Dr Dependable, I'm sure.' That was what Grant's patients had called him too, but she'd known differently. The only thing she could depend on her ex to do was cheat. Some people were very good at presenting a perfect image of themselves when underneath they were very different indeed. That said…she'd seen Lucas in action and noted the tender way he'd coaxed Mrs Templeton away. 'Where is she?'

'In the visitors' room on the ward. She's had tea, phoned her sister and is settled in watching reruns of *The Chase*.'

'Great. Thanks. I can take it from here.' Ivy started to make her way along the corridor towards the lift but was frustrated to feel Lucas Matthews's presence at her side. Worse, his scent wound round her, a mixture of something earthy and something decidedly masculine filling the air and making her belly contract with—she was horrified to realise—longing.

His jaw tightened. 'I said I'd see her, so I will.'

It was late, she was tired, and her defences were clearly wearing thin. She was struggling to ignore all her bodily reactions to this man, but if she didn't play ball, she had a feeling he'd nip at her heels anyway. 'I'm not going to get rid of you, am I?'

He pulled a face of pretend hurt. 'I'm afraid not.'

He was infuriating, but his expression made her smile. She shook her head in exasperation. 'Okay. Okay. You can come with me, but I do the talking.'

'Whatever.' He rolled his eyes but not before they glittered with amusement.

So, much against her better judgement, they both attended with Mrs Templeton, explained that Ivy had found a leaking artery from the previous surgery, that it was now cauterised, and Mr Templeton would be back home in no time.

They were rewarded with hugs and tears and the kind of gratitude that reminded Ivy why she'd chosen this career and not followed the rest of the family into the army…despite the conflict it had created between her and her parents. This job, helping people, was everything to her. Good-looking, charming colleagues notwithstanding.

Still, he made for good eye candy.

As they walked towards the hospital exit Ivy's stomach growled so loudly she put her hand to her belly, then glanced up at Lucas to see if he'd heard it.

Of course he had. The man had heard enough about her this evening to make her blush with embarrassment as she pressed her hand against her abdomen to try stop the sounds erupting from there again.

He grinned. 'Hungry?'

Another pained growl. Denying it was pointless. 'Starving. I can't remember when I last ate. Breakfast, maybe? But it's nothing a packet of noodles and a jug of boiling water won't sort out.'

He frowned. 'Two-minute noodles are not

enough nourishment after a full day's work and then an unexpected surgery. You need proper food.'

They stepped out into a cool June night. Ivy pulled her coat tight around her. 'I like noodles.'

'I know a great place that serves the best noodles in Sydney. Proper thick noodles with a decent sauce and real meat. Even vegetables and real spices, not rehydrated ones. You want to come with?'

Did she? She looked up at him and felt her belly jitter with excitement again. Er…no. That way lay only danger. She patted her laptop bag. 'I… I've still got a ton of work to do.'

'Hey. No strings. Just two colleagues eating some much-needed food after a day from hell.' He brushed his fingers through his messy hair and gave a shrug she thought he might have intended to look nonchalant, but instead made him look as if he carried the weight of the world on those broad shoulders.

'You too, huh?' She knew how it went; medicine was hard mentally and emotionally. But she'd been so hell-bent on defending her territory she hadn't stopped to think about how Lucas's day had gone or what he'd been doing before he'd found her in her office. 'Care to share?'

He shrugged. 'I lost a patient this morning. Her apartment burnt down because she'd lit a candle too close to a curtain. She evacuated safely but then went back in to try to save her cat—which, it transpires, and very tragically for my patient, was already outside. Within minutes she'd succumbed to the smoke and had burns covering ninety per cent of her body. Yesterday, she had the rest of her life to look forward to and now she's just a victim of making the wrong call at the wrong time. Makes you re-evaluate a lot, right?' After the longest sentence she'd ever heard him say he blew out a slow breath, his shoulders slumping slightly. For someone who regularly dealt with these kinds of tragedies he looked genuinely affected.

Her heart contracted. 'I hate those kinds of days.'

'Don't we all?' His eyebrows rose. 'I also had some tough news to break to another patient this afternoon. And then a run-in with this particularly fiery doctor who wants to call all the shots on a shared patient and won't even try to negotiate terms.'

'Me? Fiery? And you make it sound like a hostile business takeover.' But then, she had been reluctant to listen to his point of view.

He shrugged again, but a smile played on his lips. 'Plus, an evening trying to soothe a very concerned relative while her husband was in the operating theatre. I sat with her for ages and then the aforementioned fiery doctor didn't even want me to help out with the post-op update.'

'Way to make a girl guilt-trip.'

He was still smiling. 'Just explaining how it was from my point of view.'

Okay, she'd assumed a whole lot of things about Lucas without actually considering what was happening in his world. With a shock she noticed the shift in her perspective and a desire to know more about what made this man so infuriating on a professional level and yet so attractive on a personal one. 'I'm kind of protective about my patients.'

'I can see that, and I get it. I just hope, now we know each other a little better, we can compromise.'

'Maybe.'

He looked as if he was heading towards the staff car park, so she took this as her opportunity to leave. This emotive conversation was making her soften towards him when she should keep those hackles up.

She stopped and looked up at him. Hot damn, he was actually gorgeous. And tall. And smelt just great. Her hackles wilted as his gaze snagged hers. Had she already noticed his eyes? She'd been too blindsided by frustration and irritation to look closely. But now she took notice. Dark and soulful and beautiful.

She'd noticed his eyes. This was most definitely her cue to leave. 'Right, well, I live just round the corner, so I'll head on home. Thanks again for your help with the Templetons.'

'Last chance on the best Vietnamese food in Sydney. They do an amazing beef pho, and the lemongrass chicken noodle salad has to be eaten to be believed. I'm going regardless, makes little difference to me if you tag along.' He shrugged, his eyes glittering. 'But…you will regret for ever that you haven't tried the best pho in town.'

She wavered and clearly he saw that because he jumped in with, 'Come on, what's the harm?'

The harm was the softening towards him. The catch in her belly when he smiled. His eyes…oh, those eyes. It would be too easy to like the man. Which would go against everything she'd promised herself post-Grant, the charismatic charmer. No men. No risk of heartache. No tangle of commitment that would take months of pain to sift through and untangle.

But then her belly growled again and when Lucas bugged his eyes at her temptation got the better of her. She huffed out a breath. 'Okay. Okay. If the food is that good, I'll take a risk.'

'Good. But now you must call me Lucas, no more Dr Matthews. And I'm more than happy to give you a lift if you don't have your car here.'

'I don't, so thank you. But don't think for a minute that once I've eaten, I'll be less hangry or willing to change my mind about Emma's treatment schedule. *Lucas,*' she added with enough emphasis that said she was not going to take any nonsense from him.

'You think I'm bribing you with food? No way. How could you even think that?'

'Because you've clearly identified my weak point. I can never turn down the offer of food someone else has cooked.'

'Good to know.' He playfully wiggled his eyebrows then zapped his keys towards a flash silver e-sports car.

'Oh, you are such a stereotype.' She laughed as she climbed into the plush passenger seat, hoping that if she could keep telling herself she wasn't attracted to him, and that this was purely to fill her empty belly, then she might start believing it.

The restaurant was not at all what she'd expected. Tucked away down an alley off Dixon Street in Chinatown, it was more street food than high-end, with plastic chairs and rickety Formica-topped tables, and plumes of steam and flames billowing from the open kitchen every few minutes. The delicious aromas of star anise, ginger and garlic filled the air as a waitress showed them to their table saying, 'Hi, Dr Lucas. Good to see you again. Three nights in a row. I'm impressed.'

Ivy turned to Lucas and laughed. 'Three nights in a row? Please don't tell me you've brought a different woman here every night too?'

The waitress chuckled. 'Dr Lucas brings all his friends here.'

Which wasn't exactly the answer Ivy had been looking for.

Grinning, Lucas took both menus and handed one to Ivy as the waitress went to attend another table. 'Um… Dr Hurst? Drink?'

'Just water, please. And it's Ivy. Please, call me Ivy.' Okay, so she was softening and she just couldn't help it. She peered up at the red lanterns hanging from the ceiling casting a vibrant glow over the wood and bamboo fixtures. 'This place is amazing. How did you find it?'

'I treated Binh, the head chef, when he had a bad burn from some hot oil. Anh, our waitress and the co-owner, is his wife.'

'A family affair. Nice.'

He grimaced. 'It works well for them, but I wouldn't say that working with my family is high on my to-do list.'

'Nor mine.' When he looked at her quizzically she changed the subject, not wanting to bring the conversation down by talking about the difficulties she had with her family. 'So you recommend the pho?'

'Definitely.' He beckoned Anh back and ordered two beef pho and water then frowned as his phone began to ring.

He took it out of his pocket, frowned some more, then put it on the table face down.

Ivy watched with interest. Girlfriend? Wife? God, she didn't know anything about him. The gossip grapevine informed her he was a playboy type, but what if it was wrong? What if he was in a relationship no one knew about? Worse, what if he was no better than her ex and didn't think cheating was a crime?

She glanced at the phone then back at him. 'You can answer it, you know. I promise I won't listen. *I* don't listen in on other people's phone calls.' She hoped she'd said it with enough playful barb for him to get the message.

He grinned. 'Aw, come on. It was a small room, you had it on speaker phone, what could I do?'

'Walk away? Put your fingers in your ears?' She found herself laughing as she watched him do exactly that. 'Ugh. What did you hear?'

'That your ex is a douchebag.'

'His reputation is almost as bad as yours.' Maybe this would eke out some personal details and make her feel better about being here with him.

He spluttered. 'I have a reputation?'

'Totally. Commitment-phobe, heartbreaker.'

His dark eyes lit up. 'Excellent. Because the last thing I need is for anyone to fall in love with me.'

'Because you're already married? Engaged? In a relationship?'

'None of the above.'

'Then how big-headed can you get thinking women are bound to fall in love with you? Oh, I know all about guys like you. Grant was exactly the same, so sure of himself. Now he's free and single and let loose on the hospital staff.' She shuddered. 'Poor women. He should come with a relationship health warning.'

'Grant? He works at the Central? Do I know him?'

'Grant Nelson.'

'The urologist?' His eyebrows hiked.

'The very same.'

'How long were you together?'

'Close on five years.'

'Whoa.' He looked impressed. 'And he walked away from *you*? The mighty Ivy Hurst?'

She laughed. Sure, she was confident and knew how to call the shots in her job, but her personal life was an entirely different matter. For a while, Grant had destroyed any self-esteem she had, although she was working hard to rebuild that now. She knew her worth. Knew what she was prepared to accept in a relationship, or from a date.

'Mighty? Me? No way. He thought I was a pushover and that he could treat me like something he scraped off his shoe. But I got the last word, dumping him by text after one of my friends caught him cheating on me. Then I threw his belongings onto the front yard for him to collect. In the rain.'

'Ouch.' His phone rang again. He blinked at the sound. Ignored it.

She glanced at it. 'Please answer it, it might be important.'

'It's my mother, I highly doubt that.'

He was ignoring a call from the famous and indubitable Dr Estelle Matthews, who, alongside her husband and other sons, had built up a stellar career as a plastic surgeon to Australia's rich and famous?

Interesting. Why wouldn't he answer her call?

Ivy thought about her difficult relationship with her own parents. 'At least she's phoning you.'

The ringing stopped then the sound of an incoming text had him reaching for his phone again. He read it and frowned. 'As I thought. She wants to know who I'm bringing to her charity fundraiser.'

'And who are you bringing?' Weird that her gut did a little jolt of interest mingled with surprising disappointment at the thought of him with another woman.

He shrugged nonchalantly as if he had a long list he had to consult before making his decision. He probably had. 'I haven't decided yet.'

'So many women to choose from?'

'Far from it. Trust me, I wouldn't want to inflict anyone I actually like to an evening with my parents. They'll be asking when we're getting married, how many kids we're planning. My mother does not know the meaning of discretion.'

'She wants you married off?' This was interesting.

'Only so she can organise some big fancy wedding to show off to her society friends. She mixes in very high Sydney circles.' He rolled his eyes again. 'And is very keen on dragging me into them too.'

'I was dragged from army base to army base growing up. I know a lot about family expectations and not living up to them, but little about high society. You have a very different life from me.'

'*They* do.' He leaned back in his chair, hands clenched around the back of his head, long legs stretching under the table. As he raised his arms his shirt tugged loose from his trouser waistband giving her an enticing glimpse of bare skin. Her body rippled with a sudden need to put her fingers there.

What the hell?

She dragged her eyes up and his gaze snagged hers. A long lazy smile formed on his lips, as if he could read her thoughts. 'Me? I'm just a regular guy.'

She took in his flash suit, the smart mouth. The infuriatingly beautiful eyes that too frequently glittered with amusement at something she inadvertently said or did. The reputation. The sports car. 'Sure you are.'

'And Grant Nelson is an idiot for letting you go.'

So Lucas was a flirt too. Interesting. But despite her misgivings she was transfixed by the deep, dark brown and the flashes of gold playing across his gaze. There was something about him that was powerful and engaging. His unwavering confidence of how damned gorgeous he was, accompanied by that undercurrent of compassion, was unbelievably, mind-blowingly sexy.

Regular? You really are not.

Ivy thought about a film she'd watched when Harper had stayed with her and they'd blobbed on the sofa and eaten a bucket of ice cream. 'So, it looks like you have two options.'

'Oh?' His eyes widened and he leaned forward. 'Tell me more.'

'You either tell your mum to back off from your private life, or tell her you're involved with someone just to get her off your case.'

'Ah.' He leaned back, looking slightly deflated. What had he thought she was going to say? He'd looked very interested. *Sexually* interested. 'I can't count the number of times I've told her to stay out of my business but she's my mother, she thinks it's her duty to be *in* my personal life.'

'So, take option b. Pretend you're involved with someone.'

His eyebrows knitted together. 'That sounds a lot like a cheesy romcom movie.'

'They're the best ones. The cheesier the better. As long as the pretend partner is fully aware of the plot it'll be fine. Get someone to play along. Pay someone?'

'Might work.' He drummed his fingers on the table as he considered her suggestion. Then his eyes met hers. 'Will you do it?'

'Me? Ha, ha. No.' She faked a laugh but her belly danced at the prospect of being with Lucas at some fancy ball. All the more reason to turn him down. 'Definitely not.'

'It's one fundraiser event. Where's the harm—?' He was interrupted by Anh carrying two huge bowls of pho and their water, which she put down in front of them.

Ivy sipped a spoonful of piping-hot pho, hoping to distract him from their previous conversation. There was no way she could go to an event with him even if he paid her. 'Oh, wow. This is delicious. I love the flavours.'

He gave her a self-satisfied smile. 'Told you. But you still haven't answered my question. Will you be my pretend partner?'

CHAPTER THREE

Ugh. He hadn't been distracted. He really did want her to be his fake girlfriend. If she'd thought she'd be in this predicament she wouldn't have suggested it at all. 'No, Lucas. I won't. But I'm sure there are tons of women at work who'd take you up on the offer.'

'I'm not so sure. Besides, I'm not asking them, I'm asking you. Come with me to the ball to get my mother off my back. In return you get to show Grant Nelson that your heart is well and truly healed and he is missing so, so much.'

Interesting...

Tempting, even. 'How would Grant even find out? I doubt he'd be invited, it's not his kind of thing. And no way would anyone else ever find out about this.'

'The ball is reported in all the major newspapers. Mother makes sure of it. So, unless you wore a mask, your cover would be blown very quickly. Plus, how better for him to know how much you've moved on by seeing your picture in the media, a good-looking guy on your arm—'

'You really do have a high opinion of yourself.' Even so, she could feel herself wavering at the prospect of Grant getting a hit of jealousy.

'Okay…' A wry smile and a nod of assent. 'With a relatively passable-looking guy on your arm, dancing the night away at a glitzy charity do in a beautiful dress.'

Oh, so tempting.

How long since she'd been out dancing? She couldn't remember. Could barely remember the last time she'd been out at all. There'd been no men since Grant. The only dates she'd been on recently were ones involving just her, a bottle of wine and romcoms on her streaming service. So the prospect of a night out dancing was tempting. Hell, she only had a few months before she hit forty. She needed to increase her fun quotient before she was too old. 'When is this ball?'

'Three weeks from Saturday.'

'Okay…' Nowhere near enough time to get entangled emotionally. She would go to the ball, she would be in the papers. Grant would see it. She'd have some fun and play dress-ups in a pretty gown for a change instead of her usual green scrubs. She bit her bottom lip as she considered that the pros considerably outweighed the cons.

Lucas leaned forward and caught her gaze

again, held her captured as he teased, 'Ivy Hurst, I do believe you're tempted.'

She blinked up at him. Even though he was exactly the kind of man she'd sworn off, there was something intensely attractive about him. She had to be careful. 'And afterwards? What about…us?'

Because in the movies the pretend *us* always became a real us in the end and she had to remind herself this was not the movies.

Us.

The word slipped into her chest and filled her with heat. She imagined those hands circling her waist and him pulling her closer. Those lips on hers.

A hum tingled low in her belly. Her mouth was suddenly dry and…the thought of hot sex with Lucas made her tingle with anticipation.

Geez, she was actually living in a cheesy rom-com dream world. They were talking about a fake relationship. There would be an end…especially when there was no real beginning. No meet cute. No best-friends-to-lovers thing.

'Us?' His eyebrows rose as he considered her question. 'I would quietly announce to my family that we've decided it's not going to work. Job commitments…the usual.'

'Your usual, maybe. Not mine. And after that, we're done, that's it?'

'Absolutely. No strings.'

'No strings.' Drumming her fingers on the table, she took a chance on upping the negotiating game and playing to her advantage. 'And I get to call the shots on Emma's operation schedule.'

'Whoa. We did not agree to that.' Laughing, he leaned back and raised his hand. 'Ivy Hurst, you do not play fair.'

'I play to win.' She leaned towards him and grinned.

Gotcha.

She realised she was enjoying this sparring. There was a delicious danger in the subtext of their words. 'I like winning.'

'Luckily, I like playing. A lot.' His eyes sparked hot flashes of tease as he mused for a few moments, pursing his lips as he thought.

She imagined playing with him. And found herself shocked that she wanted to. Heat rushed through her, mixed with anticipation and excitement.

He raised his eyebrows. 'Hmm. Okay.'

'Okay as in yes? Really?' Who was being the pushover now?

He nodded assertively. 'Really.'

'Okay, then I'm in too.' Why the hell not? She was a grown woman of thirty-nine. 'It's about time I had a little fun.'

And took what she wanted for a change.

'Then we've got ourselves a deal. Shake on

it?' He held out his hand and she slipped hers into it. The sparks firing across her skin from his touch almost whipped her breath away. Her gaze shot up to his and his eyes glittered with blatant wickedness. He'd felt that shiver of desire too. And, surprising herself more than anything, she didn't shy away, she leaned into it.

Was she playing with fire? Playing to her desires, more like. She'd never felt more alive or… was it just turned on?

He let go of her hand. 'I guess we're going to need to spend some time together to get our stories straight.'

'Fine with me.' She shrugged with a smile. 'The prospect of spending a little more time with you isn't entirely onerous.'

He guffawed, then raised his glass of water. 'Glad to hear it.'

'If it means payback to my ex,' she clarified, although she was not unaware of the shiver of excitement low in her belly.

'Right. Yes. Of course.' He looked momentarily shaken then beamed a generous smile. 'I'm looking forward to getting to know you better, Ivy.'

'And you, Lucas.' Her body tingled with that kind of promise. She clinked her glass against his. The deal, she realised, involved getting to know each other in many different ways.

Whoa. What was she actually doing? Why was she feeling like this?

But she had to admit she liked it.

Heat shimmied through her as her gaze meandered over his face, then his shoulders, chest. It had been a long time since she'd felt this attracted to anyone and she grasped the feeling and held on tight.

Then as he smiled a lazy smile full of promise, she imagined dancing in his arms, pressed against that chest. The tilt of his head as he lowered his mouth to hers.

Hell. Now she was *thinking* like a cheesy romcom. This was make-believe. Her life was far from a romcom. What had she agreed to? Her defences had been battered down by a disarming smile and a chance for some revenge on her ex and to be a woman instead of just a doctor married to her career.

She put her glass down and drew her eyes away from his. Picked up her pho bowl.

Looked back at the glass rather than look up at him and let him see the excitement and confusion she knew was in her gaze.

I've only had a glass of water. This man is dangerous. What the hell would I have agreed to with a couple of wines under my belt?

'This is so good.' Ivy tipped back the bowl of pho and drank the delicious liquid.

Lucas sat back and watched. Her pure enjoyment from the food was a jolt to his equilibrium. Since when did he get a kick out of watching someone enjoy eating?

But he knew it was a lot more than that. Ivy Hurst was…surprising. Her mouth was…it sounded crazy, but her mouth was the thing of dreams. Full soft lips, a hesitancy to curve into a smile but when they did it whisked his breath away, doing weird things to his gut and firing his imagination. That mouth against his. On him. Over him.

Well, hell. This deal wasn't exactly what he'd planned. Which had, honestly, only been about getting some food with a colleague.

It was far better than that. The woman in front of him was beautiful, intelligent and very, very sexy.

His mother would love her. His father might even raise an impressed eyebrow, if he could drag himself away from his golfing cronies.

His brothers would die of envy.

His sister…oh, lovely Flora…would she like Ivy and then be distraught when the *us* became just dull old single Lucas again?

He almost wavered at that thought; he had no desire to upset his sister. But truth was, she was probably utterly uninterested in his love life.

Now he'd peeled away some of the more authoritarian layers of Ivy he wanted to get to know her a whole lot better. And not just so he could fool his parents into thinking he was settling down with a good woman. There was something about her that got to him, that had slid beneath his skin. It wasn't just her fiery protectionism for her patients or the hard work ethic, it was something else. She had a professional calm veneer that belied the warm woman she really was.

'You were right. This is an epic restaurant.' Ivy wiped that gorgeous mouth with the back of her hand. 'I can't remember when I had food that tasted so delicious.'

'So next time I suggest something, go with it, okay?'

'That sounds dangerous.' Her eyes widened with something he could only describe as delight. 'Do women always do what you say?'

'Not enough.' He shrugged. A drip of pho trickled down her chin. He couldn't help but pick up his napkin, lean over and dab it away…wishing he could do it with his tongue instead.

She blinked up at him and pulled back with a frown, her mouth forming an angry 'o' shape. Had he misread the flirting? Was this purely a platonic plan?

Are we having sex as part of this deal?

It was way too early for that. He glanced at his watch. And far too late to still be here. He called Anh over and paid the bill then scraped his chair back. 'Okay, Dr Hurst. Come on.'

She frowned again. 'Where?'

'It's late, we both need to get some sleep. I'll drop you at home.'

'Thanks.' Her shoulders sagged a little and he could see the bruising exhaustion around her eyes. She'd worked a long day and done unexpected surgery, which had made it a long evening too. 'I'm too tired to argue and you're cheaper than a taxi.'

'Me? Cheap?'

Her smile returned as she laughed. 'Not even a little bit?'

'Never. And especially not when it comes to my…um, partners.'

Her cheeks bloomed with patches of pink and her pupils grew huge. 'And why would I need to know that?'

'In case you were wondering.'

'Ha. I wasn't.'

'But you are now.'

'I am not.' She rolled her eyes, but not before he saw the flare of desire. Was she imagining them in bed together? Just how good he was?

He leaned closer to her ear. 'Oh, but you are.'

And despite her previous frowns she *was* imagining it, he was sure of it, because he saw the shiver and the slightest tilt of her body towards him. The smile playing on her lips. Felt the graze of her fingertips across his chest before she abruptly turned and walked away.

Something tugged hard and deep in his gut. He wanted her. And even though she was trying damned hard not to, she wanted him too. The chemistry was off the scale.

He followed her outside to his car, watching the cute sway of her backside, then opened her door and watched as she slid in, her soft linen skirt riding up her bare legs, showing a glimpse of thigh and perfect creamy skin. Man, she was achingly beautiful. He closed his eyes, battling back a strong urge to pick her up and carry her up to his apartment. Lay her on his bed and strip her naked.

Instead, he climbed into the driver's seat and started the engine. They drove in silence save for her giving him directions to her apartment. The night was cool, but the atmosphere in the car was thick and heavy and loaded, filled with her perfume of something flowery, maybe some citrus. And the echoes of things said and unsaid.

I like to play.

I like to win.

They could do both, right?

He pulled up outside her apartment building, a smart new block around the corner from the hospital, and went to unbuckle his seat belt, but she stopped him. 'I can manage from here. Thanks.'

'Never in my life have I let a woman walk herself to her door and I'm not going to start now.'

She shrugged. 'Oh? And a gentleman too?'

'Not all the time.' But right now, he was going to be exactly that. Even so, he followed her up the steps aching to slide his hand across the small of her back. To just touch her.

She stopped on the top step, and he waited while she dug in her bag for her key. The light from an automatic night light illuminated her features in a soft glow. She was deep in concentration as she fumbled in her large bag, a little frown hovering over those dark eyes. He wondered what was running through her mind.

Was she going to invite him in? Did she feel this connection or was he imagining it?

'Here.' Grinning, she held up her key like a prize.

'Good. Right.' He nodded. 'I'll get going, then.'

'Okay.' She nodded too. But there was something in her eyes that gave him pause. He waited.

They looked at each other far longer than appropriate for two colleagues. He wanted to ask… but didn't. Hell, how many times had he seamlessly moved from front door to bedroom? But there was something about Ivy that made him want to do the right thing…which was whatever she wanted to do. Their agreement, after all, was about a pretend relationship. Sex had never been mentioned.

She nodded again. 'Goodnight. Thanks for dinner.'

'Night, Ivy.' He turned and left her standing

there under the light with the image of her soft alluring smile burnt into his brain.

He hadn't known what he'd been expecting, but it certainly wasn't to feel this…deflated. He hadn't realised just how much he'd wanted to spend more time with her. How much the prospect of getting to know her better had resonated with his mind and his libido.

He took a couple of steps down then heard, 'Lucas. Wait.'

He turned, his heart hammering. 'Yes?'

She held her key up again. 'Do you want to come in?'

She'd bantered with him, flirted with him and met him match for match, but when he'd dabbed her chin with his napkin she'd leaned away. He sure as heck wasn't going to assume anything. 'Why?'

'Hmm.' She bit her bottom lip. 'The thing is, I don't do this. I don't take impromptu dates. I don't make rash deals with dangerous men.'

'If anything is dangerous it's your damned smile.' He laughed. 'You have so got the wrong impression of me.'

'Oh, I think I've worked you out.' She drummed her fingers over her pretty lips. 'But tonight has been very out of my comfort zone and I've agreed to some ridiculous plan with an almost stranger.'

'Hey. You know where I work. We've had dinner. We've saved a guy's life and comforted his wife together. We've even had a stand-up row. I never usually get to that part of a relationship.'

'Why am I not surprised?' She giggled. 'I'm trying to work out if you're a good influence or a bad one.'

'I can be whichever one you want. But let it be noted that *you* convinced *me* to lie to my parents. *You* are the one seeking revenge on your ex. I'm just an innocent bystander.'

'Innocent?' She closed her eyes and put her palms together. 'Please, God, don't let him be innocent.'

Then she looked up at him, and her expression became…curious. Playful. So damned sexy. He saw her eyes darken, the soft dart of her tongue to wet her lips. Something passed between them. That connection again. An implicit understanding.

I see you. I want you.

He stepped closer. He couldn't not.

Without breaking eye contact and with blatant desire in her gaze she rose up on tiptoe and put her hand to his cheek.

Then her mouth was on his.

CHAPTER FOUR

He inhaled sharply at the shock of her move but cupped her face and pulled her closer. Because it was the only possible response. And if he'd thought she might be cautious or coy he'd been wrong. Very wrong. She was as assured as he was, if not more so. She tasted salty from the pho and achingly sweet. She was hot and soft and yielding and he wanted to sink right in.

She bunched his shirt in her fist, moaning as he took the kiss deeper. And that sound was almost the undoing of him. He snaked an arm around her waist and pulled her closer, feeling the crush of her breasts against his chest, the press of her hip against his thigh.

This was not part of their deal. But it was the very best part of it all. Even though it was also a little crazy. This wasn't a one-night-stand arrangement. They would have to get to know each other if they were going to fool his family, and that meant getting his head in the game too, not just his body. He didn't do that. Not ever.

But separate his brain from this kind of action? No, thank you.

Her key clattered to the floor, making her jump away from him. 'Damn.'

Damn indeed. A sign from the gods that this wasn't meant to be?

Her breathing came faster, her eyes almost greedy with need as she bent and patted the ground trying to find her key. She straightened, brandishing it. 'Come in, Lucas.'

He remembered her earlier retort and gave it back to her as he rested his forehead against hers, breathing in her delicate scent and wanting to be covered in it. 'Do men always do what you ask?'

'Not enough.' She shrugged in a bad imitation of himself.

He laughed. 'Well, I don't need asking twice.'

He grasped her hand and let her lead him inside, through a too-bright communal hallway, up the stairs to the first floor and into her kitchen.

He imagined her apartment was neat and tidy, and that there were no dishes draining on the sink. That any spilt crumbs had been efficiently wiped away the moment they'd been made. That it was decorated in feminine shades. He imagined her home to be like her; efficiently contained with soft edges.

But there was no opportunity to confirm his suspicions. His eyes were only on her. On the back of her neck. On the soft fabric of her blouse, the outline of her bra strap. Was this happening? Was this for real?

He thought she might stall and offer him the obligatory drink. But, instead, she threw her key onto a white painted table in the centre of the room, then turned and kissed him hard again.

There was that throaty sound again, making him hard and hot. He walked her backwards and pinned her against the kitchen wall, the kiss deepening into something feral and wild. He slid his hand up her blouse, laughing softly as she shuddered at his touch. He cupped her breast, first over then under her bra and she curled against him, whimpering into his mouth.

He shoved off her coat, removed her blouse, unclipped her bra and then bent to suck a perfect nipple into his mouth. She writhed against him, fingers in his hair. 'That is so good.'

'We haven't even started.' He slicked a trail of kisses up her throat and back to capture her mouth in another mind-melting wet kiss. Her hands skimmed his body, tugging his shirt from his waistband and unbuttoning. She threw the shirt onto the floor then her hands explored his chest, arms, shoulders.

'Nice. You work out, Dr Matthews?'

'Kite surfing mostly, when I get the chance.'

She slid her palms over his biceps, her eyes glittering with tease. 'I've always fancied doing that and even signed up for a lesson once, but chickened out at the last minute.'

'You should do it. It's the best thing ever. Like you're flying and harnessing the wind. It's a real buzz.' He loved that she was so casual and not self-conscious. That they could learn about each other in all these different ways.

Just to fool his family, he reminded himself. Then this deal was finished. Done. But until then…

She cupped his face and laughed. 'I can see the excitement in your eyes.'

'Trust me, any excitement you see right now has nothing to do with kite surfing.' He stole another kiss as he slid his hands down past her waist and unzipped her skirt. It fell in a pool at her feet.

She stepped out of it, leaving her naked but for a pair of white lace panties. 'A surf bum, huh? Not a reader of the classics or a social justice warrior. There are no hidden depths here.'

She reached up and tousled his hair then ran her fingers down over his cheek, to his throat. She traced a line down his chest, which she then followed with her tongue. Lower. Lower.

He thought he was going to go insane with need. He was going to lose it.

He put his hand to her cheek and brought her back to look at him. She thought she had the measure of him, which clearly gave her a rush of power, which he liked. And true, he liked to surf. Liked a beer. Liked women. No harm done. He grinned before he caught her mouth again.

And kept the fact that he actually set himself a book-reading target each year, which included at least two classics. That he'd spent the last few years trying to convince his parents to offer pro bono work at their swanky clinic. But he let her run with the all-brawn fantasy because it suited him too. 'You got me. I'm such an Aussie cliche. For my sins. Of which there are many.'

She kissed his neck. 'Good.'

'Good that I have many sins? Or good that I'm a surf bum?'

'All of the above. The last thing I need is a complicated, deep-thinking man who takes life too seriously. Let's keep it simple.'

'Simply sex. At your service.' He did a mock doff of his cap.

She caught his hand and slid one of his fingers into her mouth, which had him wishing it were other body parts there in that silky soft cocoon.

Then he couldn't bear it any longer, he had to taste her again in a long, hot kiss that seared his brain and made him so damned hard he wanted to sink deep inside her. He lifted one of her legs and she wrapped it around his backside. He fitted in between her legs as if he was meant to be there.

But she pulled back, her mouth slightly open,

her lips swollen and pink. Looking impossibly sexy and mussed-up. Her hair, normally a perfect straight bob, was unruly and dishevelled. She was as undone as he was.

She put her hand on his hip, slid her fingers along his waistband. 'I am way too old for up-against-the-wall sex. The bedroom's through here.'

He laughed but again let her take him by the hand and lead him into the bedroom, where she pushed him onto the bed, slid his trousers off and climbed on top of him, straddling his thighs.

He lay there, his hands stroking her thighs, looking up into beautiful eyes that were commanding and dark but with a hint of…vulnerability? Caution? As if she wasn't quite as convinced by her act as she wanted to be. And some of it was an act, he was sure. Because he'd seen her at work. He'd seen the compassion and caring. He'd seen her answer an emergency with authority yet humanity. There were depths in her professional life, so there would surely be some in her personal one too.

Whatever. If she just wanted uncomplicated sex, he was her man. He stepped his fingertips up her thighs. 'Ivy Hurst. You like to be on top?'

'I like… Oh.' She shuddered as he slid his finger inside her. She was so hot and wet and ready for him. 'I like that. Very much.'

'I want to be inside you. Right now.' He

couldn't get over the way they'd just clicked after all that antagonism. Couldn't get his head around the deal they'd made. And now this. It was like a dream. A fantasy. He'd gone from calling her 'Dr Hurst' in clipped tones to purring 'Ivy' against her neck in a matter of hours and she was about to ride him.

'Oh, no. Not yet.' She slid her palm over his trousers against the rock of erection, her eyes misted with desire, a sexed-up smile on her lips.

He slid his finger inside her again. Then another.

Leaning in and kissing him, she freed him. Took him in her hand and stroked long delicious pulls that made him moan in pleasure.

The faster she stroked, the faster he slid his fingers until she was pulsing against him. 'Lucas…that is…' She closed her eyes.

'Look at me. Ivy, *look* at me. I want to watch you.'

Her eyes flickered open and she looked directly at him as she rocked hard against his fingers. Then he felt her tighten and suck in fast shuddering breaths before she threw her head back and moaned, 'Oh. My. God. Lucas.'

The way she said his name was like a prayer and the punch of it slid under his ribcage and arrowed directly to his groin. He pushed her hand away from his erection before it was all over, before it properly began. 'Geez, Ivy. You are so freaking hot.'

'Thank you.' She fell forward, looking almost drunk on the orgasm, and kissed him. 'And you are excellent.'

'Condom?'

She shook her head, her features softened. 'Hot damn. No. I threw them all out.'

'Into the yard with the rest of his stuff?'

'Yes.' She shrugged ruefully. 'But I very much regret my rashness now.'

'Lucky I have one, then.' He stretched to the edge of the bed, reached down to his trouser pocket and fished out his wallet. Grabbed the foil and tore it open. Laughed as she helped him wiggle out of his boxers.

She grinned too, pursing her lips. 'You always carry condoms? You get that much sex?'

He guffawed. 'I'd like to get that much sex.'

'Me too.' She smiled, rubbing her cheek against his. 'Lots and lots of sex.'

'So when you said you were off men...'

'Whoa, whoa, whoa.' She bit her bottom lip and grinned. 'I didn't mean I was off sex. Or orgasms. The more of them, the merrier. Please.'

Man, she was funny, beautiful, hard core. He laughed. 'Then we'd better make a start.'

The mood got serious as he sheathed and slid her forward on his thighs, positioning his erection at her entrance. She bent and kissed him, and he cupped her breasts, soft and beautiful in his hands. Her mouth hot and wet. He didn't think he'd ever been so hard. It was taking all his strength not to explode right then and there.

This was Ivy freaking Hurst. Some kind of crazy dream.

And he didn't want to wake up.

Ivy inhaled as she lowered onto him, every nerve ending tingling with the last vestiges of her orgasm, but she was hungry for more.

Lucas's hands skimmed her waist and tugged her forward a little, raising her up on her shins. She sank down on him again, watching his beautiful face crease into ecstasy. She was doing this to him. She was making him wild with need.

But, *whoa.* This wasn't who she was.

She didn't have sex with someone she barely knew. She didn't take what she wanted. She didn't play. But here she was, doing just that. And she was loving this new version of herself.

He raised his hips and thrust inside her and her thoughts blurred. She clung onto now, to this. Sensation after sensation…an intense physical pleasure and something more…a catch in her heart as she looked at his face. A knowing as their eyes locked.

Look at me.

She couldn't look away.

She slid up his length and then sank slowly

over him again. He groaned, deep and hoarse, then moved his hips in time with her slow rhythm.

She leaned forward and pressed her palms into his shoulders as his pace quickened into long, greedy thrusts. She tried to hold onto the sensations, to grasp each one as it rippled through her…the taste of him, the feel of him. The stirring in her belly, the ache for more of this. The blush of her skin under his gaze.

There were so many sensations coming so fast she let herself fall into them, into the long, fast strokes. Into the bright light in his eyes, then the clouding with pure pleasure. The rub of his palm, the wet of his mouth. The scruff of his hair against her chest bone. She fell and she fell and she fell. Faster. Harder. Until she felt his grip on her arms tighten and, as he called her name into the darkness, she shattered into a million pieces.

She closed her eyes, finally releasing herself from his hold.

Whatever demons she'd been exorcising were well and truly erased.

More, she'd probably made a deal with the devil and was likely going to hell for encouraging him to lie to his family. But she didn't regret a moment.

Not a single one.

Lucas lay back, cradling her against his chest and waiting for the buzz to fade. When he could finally manage to form words he admitted, 'Ivy, I lied to you.'

Her body stiffened and she looked up at him, frowning. 'You did what? Please tell me you're not in a relationship. I hate cheaters.'

'Hey, no way. I'm not. I told you that kite surfing was the best thing ever, but I think Ivy sex tops it.' He pressed a kiss on her cheek. 'You're my new favourite hobby.'

Geez. Cheesy? He didn't know. Didn't know much right now, his brain had been drained of anything sensible and all he wanted to do was wait five minutes then sink into her again.

She giggled. 'I think I prefer knitting, but you'll do as a second option. You know, when I get bored of knit one purl one.'

He looked around the pristine bedroom. Nothing out of place. A walk-in closet, door closed. An old-fashioned chair with a blue-cushioned window seat. No evidence of any kind of hobbies…of anything, other than sleeping. Not even a book on the nightstand. But there were some cool black and white photograph prints of twisty trees on the walls. 'You knit? I just can't imagine that. Nana.'

She laughed. 'Hey, it's actually a very cool thing to do. But, in reality, I don't have time. I used to have lots of hobbies…horse riding, yoga, thrift shopping…but now all I do is work. So you don't need to find out much more about me to tell your parents. Just say I'm a workaholic.'

'You really do need to spend your time more wisely.'

'Probably. I just sank all my energy into my career when Grant left. Which I know was a mistake, but it was a really good distraction. You got any ideas?'

'Lots.' He stroked a fingertip over her hip and pulled her close, spooning round her, already planning which position he'd like to try next. 'Well, at least I know what your apartment looks like. You have good taste in art—Mother would like that.'

She twisted round to face him, elbow bent, propping her head up in her hand. 'You're going to mention my photographs of eucalypts?'

'Well, I can't exactly tell her how good you are in bed or what your kisses are like, can I? For the record, they are mind-blowing. But wait, actually, are they? I need to double-check.' He took her face in both hands and slid his mouth over hers, losing himself in her taste and the feel of her in his arms. When he finally came up for air his chest felt as if it had been bathed in warm honey. 'No. I cannot tell her about your kisses. But I can mention that you have a jungle of houseplants.'

'Don't forget the ones outside too.' Her eyes darted to the floor-to-ceiling blinds behind which, he assumed, was a ranch slider door and her balcony.

'Out there?'

She nodded. 'My deck stretches all the way round to my lounge too, so I get afternoon and evening sun. I wouldn't want to live anywhere I couldn't sit outside. My potted plants are my pride and joy. Does that make me sound old? I mean, my days of clubbing until dawn are well and truly over.' She shuddered and laughed. 'Thirty-nine is ancient, right?'

'Not as old as me. You're just wise now and want different things. Wise people know that plants make the world a better place. Green-fingered.' He sucked in air as she ran her fingers up his thigh and cupped his burgeoning erection. He kissed the crook of her neck. 'Oh, you have multi-talented fingers.'

'And your talents are what, Dr Matthews?'

'Other than spectacular kisses and amazing lovemaking?'

Her eyebrows rose as if she was calling him out. 'Anything I can actually mention in front of your mum?'

He pursed his lips as he thought about the deal again. About having to make a pretence in front of his family. That didn't make him feel good, despite how necessary. It had seemed an easy plan when they'd discussed it in the restaurant, but now he wasn't so sure.

He liked Ivy and had a bad feeling he might regret this whole agreement if things didn't turn out how they'd planned.

He liked her and was having sex with her and had committed to being in a pretend relationship with her for the next few weeks.

What could possibly go wrong?

Everything.

He turned his attention back to her and kept his tone light. 'I make damned fine coffee.'

'That's your job for tomorrow morning, then.' Then she winced. 'I mean…you don't have to stay, obviously. Only, work is just round the corner and…' She grimaced. 'Ugh. I'm not sure on our boundaries here. My last relationship was five years. He stayed. Until he didn't.'

Lucas didn't know how to answer this. Did he want to stay the night? Go to sleep here, with her? Wake up with her in the morning? Make her coffee? Play happy couples? Pretend on top of pretend?

It wasn't something he ever did. All the women he'd dated knew the score: he wasn't going to stick around. It was always, *always* only temporary. He could not give himself, he could not love someone. He would never be responsible for anyone else's life, happiness or trust.

And yet…his chest contracted at the thought of leaving Ivy.

Geez, if that wasn't the biggest reason to hot-foot it out of here, he didn't know what was. He needed to get a grip.

He kissed the tip of her nose, avoiding any statement that sounded like either a commitment or a brush-off. 'I do need to go home and get a change of clothes and some other stuff for work.'

She blinked and nodded. 'Okay. Yes.'

And was he mistaken or did she look almost relieved at that? He wasn't sure he liked that either. Which meant he should probably leave right now.

Five more minutes.

The thought of getting out of this bed was very depressing. 'Hey, why did you pull away when I wiped the pho from your chin earlier?'

She grimaced. 'Sorry. But that's exactly the kind of thing Grant used to do. Treat me like I was a child, or a pet. I'm a grown woman.'

'You're hard core.' He cupped her backside and pulled her closer. 'But I get it. My little sister would hate it if I did that to her too. She'd also hate it if I called her little. She thinks I treat her like a baby. And she's probably right, but she's my kid sister. It's my job to protect her.'

And he'd failed. So badly.

Ivy smiled. 'How old is she?'

'Twenty-eight.'

'Oh? So not a baby at all. How old are you?'

'Forty-one.'

Her eyes narrowed and he guessed she was doing the maths. 'That's a big age difference.'

'Mum and Dad had three boys in quick succession. I'm the youngest son. Then there was a long gap…probably while she got her head around having three boys to run around after. Flora was my mum's last-chance baby. I think she was hoping for maybe Flora and one more so they could grow up together, but the one more never happened. So, Flora was our pet.'

Until he'd ruined it all. Ruined her. Ruined everything. A startling reminder that he was no good being responsible for people.

His chest constricted and familiar self-loathing rushed through him. He shifted away from Ivy. 'Anyway. I won't stay tonight, thank you. We both need a decent sleep before work tomorrow.'

'And then what?'

The six-billion-dollar question. Normally he'd leave with no plans for another date but things were different here. Not only were they going to see each other at work, but they had a deal. 'We probably should catch up some time to discuss strategy going forward.'

She pressed her lips together as if holding in a laugh. And if she noted his rapid change of subject, she didn't show it. 'Strategy. Yes. Okay.'

'Saturday? Unless you're on call?'

She nodded. 'Saturday works. I'll make sure to message you about Emma's timeline too.'

'Great.' Back to work conversations. Good. He knew how to navigate those.

Where he was struggling was that he did not know how to navigate the warm and excited feelings in his chest at the thought of spending more time with Ivy Hurst.

CHAPTER FIVE

WHAT THE HELL had they done?

What the hell was she doing?

Ivy played with the handle on her Americano coffee cup and thought about last night.

Trouble was, she couldn't stop thinking about last night. Because this was what she did: second-guessed herself. And she was currently second-guessing the one good thing that had happened to her in years.

They were two consenting adults. It shouldn't matter to anyone else what they were doing in private together. If it felt right, and hurt no one else, then, hell, she should immerse herself in it and enjoy every second.

She sighed. It had been very good sex. Lucas had been surprisingly good.

'Morning, Ivy. Sorry I'm late.' Phoebe wrapped her in a warm hug then sat down across from her in one of the huge chesterfield sofas in Perc Up, the little cafe bar across the road from the hospital. Then she put her takeaway coffee cup on the table and grinned. 'Wow, you look…happy.'

'I am.' Ivy grinned back.

'Okay. Spill. What—or rather who—has put that smile on your face?'

Ivy lowered her voice so any nearby hospital staff couldn't overhear, although that was unlikely given the way the seating was arranged in cosy huddles with tables separated from other customers by palms and potted vines. It was like an indoor garden and the perfect place for sharing secrets. 'I had sex with Lucas Matthews last night.'

Phoebe almost choked on her coffee. 'Sorry, I think I'm going deaf. I thought you said you had *sex*. With Lucas Matthews. Reconstructive surgeon.'

A delicious wave of pride and lust prickled through Ivy. 'I did.'

Phoebe tapped the table. 'I knew it! I knew there was a man in your office. What the heck, Ivy? What's going on? I thought you didn't like him.'

'I didn't know him. I did that jumping-to-conclusions thing, assuming stuff about him when I didn't know him. He's actually…well, he's kind of hot.'

'There are plenty of hot men at work, but you don't have sex with them. What happened?'

'Um…well. We had an argument. Then an

emergency. Then a debrief. Then dinner. Then I was…debriefed. Literally.' Ivy giggled. Oh, hell. She was giggling about a man. Since when did she do that?

Phoebe just gaped at her, blinking. 'Slowly. Tell me slowly.'

'Okay.' Ivy tried to control her dancing heartbeat. 'He came to my office to talk about Emma, and we got into a bit of a fight about her theatre schedule. Then one of my post-op patients turned up. Collapsed. Leaking artery. Theatre… et cetera… Then I had dinner with Lucas because he knows a great place and two-minute noodles aren't enough.' She sighed. This was far too much detail and yet she couldn't stop talking about it. And it made no sense and yet made complete sense. 'Then I agreed to be his fake girlfriend for a charity ball. And we went back to my place.'

Even now, saying it out loud sounded like something from a movie. This wasn't her life.

Phoebe shook her head, blinking rapidly. 'You did…what? I can't keep up.'

'It was awesome. All of it. And we've got another date planned for Saturday.'

'Whoa. So, for real? You slept with Lucas Matthews?' Phoebe's eyes widened and she looked suitably chastised when Ivy glared at her to quieten the heck down. 'And you're going to do it again?'

'Only until the ball, then we're done.' To be fair, they hadn't discussed whether sex would be part of it, but, after last night, she hoped so.

Phoebe shook her head. 'I have no words.'

Ivy chuckled, her post-sex glow keeping her mood buoyant, despite the fleeting second-guessing. 'Phoebe, you always have words.'

'I'm in shock. After Grant I thought…you said only last night…'

'I have well and truly exorcised Grant from my body and my mind.'

Phoebe's eyes grew huge, and she shifted uncomfortably in her seat. 'Talking of…incoming, on your left. Um…'

'What? Have you developed aphasia?' Then her friend's words sank in. 'Is he behind me? Is he…?' Lucas was here? Well, why not? This was the cafe closest to the hospital and many of her colleagues mainlined the fabulous coffee. She whirled round, excited and anxious and perturbed and turned on all at the same time, to come face to face with… 'Grant. Oh.'

Typical that her ex frequented this place too. Her excitement fizzled into frank irritation.

'Ivy.' Grant pressed a kiss to her cheek. 'What a coincidence. You look…well, you look amazing.'

'Please don't do that, Grant.' Ivy stood, not tall enough to make a physical impression but hopefully with enough gravitas to send him away.

But, as always, Grant couldn't read her. How had she wasted half a decade of her life on him?

He stepped back, his gaze sweeping her from head to toe. 'What? I'm only saying what I see. You look…ethereal.'

'Don't kiss me again, Grant. Ever. I'm not your pet, or your child, and I'm certainly not your girlfriend.'

'Oh. I…' he spluttered. 'I just wanted—'

'What?' He'd cheated on her, humiliated her, broken her. And now he wanted to pass the time of day?

'I just came in to grab a coffee and there you are, looking amazing. And I thought…' He grimaced. 'Maybe we should have a catch-up. Maybe dinner?'

The gall of him. It was bad enough having to work in the same hospital and risk running into him every day, but catch up with dinner? No way.

She thought about last night and how much fun she'd had…how unburdened she'd felt. How free, for the first time in ages, just to be herself. The way Lucas had been interested in her and made her laugh and made her feel wanted and interesting.

And the sex…

'Grant, unless you have some work thing to discuss I'd prefer it if you didn't speak to me at all. We're done.' She grabbed her bag and made a play of hauling the strap up to her shoulder as if she were about to leave.

He watched her, his shoulders slumping, eyes shifting between Ivy and Phoebe. Finally, he took the hint. 'Don't go on my account. I'll head off. Bye, Phoebe.'

Phoebe pressed her lips together as if holding in a laugh then just about managed, 'Bye, Grant.'

He turned to go then whirled back to Ivy. 'You really do look amazing.'

Her patience ran right out. 'Grant—'

'I know,' he interrupted her, looking sheepish for the first time in his life. 'I'm sorry. For everything.'

'Good.' She turned away from him, sat down and counted to ten, then sagged and whispered to Phoebe, 'Has he gone yet?'

'The door is just closing behind him. He's walking up the street.' She whistled. 'I don't think he'll be bothering you again and definitely not kissing you. Way to go, girl. You were epic. And he's right, you do look…different. Ethereal, yes. Your eyes are shining, your skin is glowing. Sex suits you.'

'Good sex suits me. Lucas sex. Not Grant sex.'

Phoebe laughed. 'Who are you and what have you done with Ivy?'

'She's having fun for the first time in for ever.'

'I'm pleased for you. Honestly. But seriously…' Phoebe patted Ivy's hand. 'Be careful.'

'We're using contraception, if that's what you mean.' She made a mental note to pop by the pharmacy on the way home and get more supplies in case this became a regular thing.

Her tummy tightened at the thought. Saturday couldn't come soon enough.

'We both know that no contraception is one hundred per cent safe.' Phoebe rolled her eyes. 'But what I meant was be careful with your heart.'

'My heart will not be involved here. It's a temporary thing to get his mum off his back. We both know the score. It's a deal where we both win, and I've already got the one benefit I was hoping for.'

'Great sex?'

'Well, that and the fact Grant now knows exactly what he's missing.'

'He really does. But you trust too easily, Ivy. You give yourself. I don't want you hurt again. Grant did a real number on you, and it's taken you a long time to get over him. I don't want you opening yourself to that again.'

'I am walking into this with my eyes wide open.' *Look at me...* Her skin was suffused with heat at the memory. It felt as if she'd dreamt it, if not for the delicious aches in places she'd almost forgotten existed. 'This is something I'm doing for me. A self-esteem boost. No regrets.'

But Phoebe's smile was filled with concern. 'Okay. But I'm here for you. Always.'

'I know. Thank you. I'll be fine. Just fine.' Ivy's beeper began to vibrate. She looked at it and grimaced. 'Shoot. My reg needs to talk to me and it's not even starting-work time yet.'

'Yes, I need to get going too.' Phoebe stood. 'I almost managed to drink a whole cup of coffee this time. I'd call that a win.'

But Ivy's head was already back at the hospital, with her work and the chances of running into a particular surgeon who kissed like a god and made her feel better than she had in years.

Up on the ward Ivy caught up with her junior doctor, Samreen, who filled her in on the latest developments with Emma before they went to see her. 'The abdominal pain's getting worse and we can't seem to get on top of it.'

'Did we get the scan done last night?'

Samreen pressed her lips together and sighed. 'No. The on-call were busy with emergency work and they haven't had a chance. They've promised to do it first thing this morning.'

'It needs to be urgent. Give them another call and chase them up, please.' Ivy shook her head. Things weren't adding up with Emma. 'Babies are okay?'

Samreen tapped on the desk computer and searched for reports. 'Obstetric ultrasound yesterday reports nothing unusual. Both babies are doing fine despite the trauma poor Mum's endured.'

'Okay. Good. It's difficult dealing with a twin pregnancy and such bad injuries from the fire, we have to make sure we keep an eye on everything. Any other symptoms?'

'No diarrhoea. Vomited three times this morning.'

'Okay. As far as I'm aware she hasn't had any other episodes of vomiting prior to this. The pain's getting worse, you say?'

'Yes.' Samreen looked at the charts she was holding. 'But she's on high-dose analgesics for her burns so the pain only shows up when her meds are wearing off.'

Ivy was coming to a conclusion she didn't want to have to draw, but it was like putting pieces of a difficult jigsaw together. 'I'll examine her again and see if we can work out what's happening. This poor woman has had multiple injuries and surgeries and is heavily pregnant, so there are lots of potential causes of abdominal pain. But the vomiting is new, so that's my biggest concern at this stage.'

Samreen nodded and scanned Emma's chart again. 'Blood results have just come in and her white cell count is creeping up. But that could be infection of a wound site, IV access or anything really. Even a UTI.'

Ivy always liked to use these kinds of conundrums as a teaching moment. 'Indeed. And the nausea and vomiting could be a side effect of her meds. But, if a normally healthy woman came in with temperature, right-radiating lower abdominal pain and vomiting, what would be your first thought?'

Samreen tapped her fingers on the desk as she thought. 'Possibly appendicitis.'

'Yes.' The unwanted conclusion Ivy was coming to. 'What do we think the chances of appendicitis are here?'

Her junior shrugged. 'About as much chance as any other person, I guess.'

'Exactly. And if it looks like a duck and talks like a duck, it's probably a duck, right?'

'Yes.'

'But it doesn't pay to jump to conclusions. If you could chase that scan, I'll check to see if there are any theatres free this afternoon, just in case. I know she's been enjoying trying to eat and drink small amounts but let's keep her nil by mouth.'

'Oh? Is that Emma's chart?' Lucas's deep voice had her whirling round while her heart did a strange little jig.

He smiled. 'Hey, Ivy.'

'Hi, Lucas.' Ivy's belly contracted at the sight of him. That smiling mouth that had given her so much pleasure. Those hands. That man. She'd straddled him and now here she was trying to act normal. Her cheeks heated and she wondered exactly how much her body was giving away to her patients and colleagues.

That would not do. She was far too old to be thinking like this and swooning over a guy. And it was bad enough she had to dodge Grant, she didn't need to add Lucas to the avoid-at-work list.

Samreen handed him the chart. 'She's not doing so well today. We think she might have appendicitis.'

'Ah. I see.' He frowned and looked back to Ivy. 'On top of everything else?'

Ivy slid her hands into her pockets, more to stop herself from reaching out and touching him than anything else. 'Her symptoms point to it, but it could be one of a few things. We're going through a process of elimination until the abdo scan results come through.'

His expression flattened. 'Any problems with the babies?'

'As far as we know there are two happy little bunnies in there. It's like doing a game of pin the symptoms to the illness, but appendicitis would explain the shooting temps, high blood cell count and vomiting.'

'Geez. As if she hasn't had enough to deal with. Is nothing going to go right for her?' Once again, he looked genuinely concerned. Every time she saw Lucas deal with a patient she was impressed by his compassionate approach, but the way he treated Emma, fought for her...well, that was personal. Why? 'If it is appendicitis then at least I know I can fix that.'

'And then I can fix the grafts.' He bugged his eyes at her and laughed.

She rolled her eyes back at him. 'Give me time to get things under control.'

'Of course.' His voice was sing-song. 'Look at us negotiating like adults. Okay if I have a word with her?'

'Absolutely. I haven't seen her yet today either, so I'll come over too.' She smiled to herself. Yes, they were negotiating. Miracles did happen. The sex had definitely helped, but it was essential she kept that completely private and away from her professional life.

If only she could stop thinking about the way he'd kissed her up against her kitchen wall.

'Hi, Emma, how are you doing today?' His tone was completely different from the way he spoke to Ivy. When he talked to patients, he was calm and concerned and yet authoritative. She thought about the way he'd groaned against her throat and called her name when he'd come. Her cheeks heated again.

Saturday.

Would it be a rerun of last night, or would it be awkward?

Emma's face crumpled as she slowly ran her

hand over her swollen belly. She was ashen, with dark circles under her eyes and exhaustion from fighting for herself and her babies written deep over her face. 'Not so good, Doc. I've got sore guts today.'

'Those babies kicking too hard?'

'I don't mind that.' Emma smiled and despite the pain Ivy could see so much mother's love there. 'I just wish they'd kick a different part. It makes me feel really sick.'

'Well, I've never been pregnant so I can't say I speak from experience…' Lucas flashed a very handsome smile at Emma '…but that doesn't sound great to me. But don't worry, Dr Hurst here is on the job and I know she'll get you sorted out. Then we can get your grafts sorted and you back home, where you belong. No one wants to be in hospital if they can help it. Not even me.'

'I'll bet.' Emma gave a slightly pathetic-sounding laugh. 'You got family waiting for you at home?'

He blinked quickly. 'Just an empty flat. Though I do have siblings, parents…'

Emma nodded, understanding the context. No wife. No kids.

Ivy thought about the way he'd spoken about his family last night with barely any emotion, certainly lacking in affection, apart from the brief softening at the mention of his sister. And how he'd chosen not to speak to his mother when she'd called. She understood how family dynamics could be difficult. Hell, communication with her parents and siblings was minimal…but, even so, her mother was the lynchpin and everyone's news was passed on by her to each of them.

But Lucas had been almost disparaging, and he'd clammed up about his sister, steering the conversation into a different direction. He wasn't exactly the clamming-up type, which meant Lucas had hidden depths.

That wasn't exactly something she wanted to know.

She'd noted the softness in his tone when he'd spoken of Flora, then the quick diversion and an altogether different tone, kind of matter of fact. But whatever he'd been trying to do hadn't worked on her because she saw something in his eyes that he couldn't wipe away with just a change of subject. Something about his sister that made him wary, or sad or…she couldn't put her finger on it. Uncomfortable? No. He clearly loved his sister. But something had happened between them.

Had he been jealous of her sudden appearance when he was what…? Thirteen? Had his parents turned all their attention away from the boys?

She couldn't work out what was affecting him, but she was good at jigsaw puzzles. She'd get there in the end.

But why? Why did it matter anyway? Working

him out would only mean she knew him better. And that way lay danger. It was easier not to get involved if she thought of him as purely physical.

'Excuse me, can I get through, please?' The sonographer pushed her way past Ivy, making her jump. She'd been in a dream world.

Her heart thumped hard against her chest. She could not let him derail her work. Ever. There was a definite line between her job and her private life. Between keeping things simple and getting deeply involved with a totally unsuitable man. With any man. Hadn't she promised herself she'd never run that risk again? So why was she trying to work him out?

She moved back to allow the sonographer some room. 'I'll be over by the nurses' station when you're done. Thanks.' Ivy nodded a smile towards Emma. 'Once we've got the results of the scan we can make a plan. In the meantime, just try and rest up. If you need anything use the call bell and we'll try to make you as comfortable as possible.'

Ivy turned to Lucas. 'I'll be in touch about the scan.'

Then she walked to the nurses' station and took some deep breaths to help her refocus on her job.

'So, Saturday.' His voice was close to her ear and the little hairs on her neck prickled to attention.

So much for the deep breaths because her whole body inclined towards him as if there were some kind of super-magnetic field around him and she were a battered old nickel unable to resist the attraction.

She turned and was barely an inch away from his mouth. It would have taken the tiniest of stretches to slide her lips over his. Heat rushed through her, pooling low in her belly. 'Yes? The deal. Yes. Right. The plan.'

She emphasised the last word to remind them both that this was about having a good cover story for his mum, and some very simple, albeit mind-blowing, sex.

Nothing else.

'The plan. Yes. I'll pick you up early. Say, eight?'

'In the morning? On my day off? You're joking, right?'

He leaned closer and whispered, 'You won't regret it. I promise.'

Almost shaking with need, Ivy glanced around, but for once all the staff were busy in cubicles and with patients, no one to notice their proximity. She stared up into those mesmerising eyes. 'I won't?'

'Not at all.' His smile was deliciously teasing. 'Wear long trousers. A jacket. It might get cold.'

'Why?'

'That would spoil the surprise.' He winked and

turned away, then added loudly, 'Let me know asap about Emma.'

'Oh, I will.' And hot damn, with just one conversation all her promises had dissolved. She wanted him.

Saturday definitely could not come soon enough.

CHAPTER SIX

WAITING FOR SATURDAY morning had Lucas feeling like a kid on Christmas Eve with the promise of a present if he went to sleep.

But sleep had been elusive these past few nights because he'd relived that one evening with Ivy over and over. He still couldn't get over how it had gone from antagonism to bed so quickly.

He wanted to do it again. Even the antagonism and arguing. That had been weirdly, sexily fun too.

And here was the thing: he didn't do this. He didn't think about a woman to the point of sleeplessness. Didn't plan future dates. Certainly didn't call on favours from old mates he hadn't seen for months just so he could make a woman smile.

But here she was, grinning wildly as they parked up at his friends' acreage property on the edge of Kung Gai National park, as he pointed out the two horses all saddled up and waiting by the timber stable block. That giddy smile gave him the best gut punch of pride he'd ever had.

Her eyes sparkled as the reality of their next few hours dawned. 'Horse riding?'

'No. Airplane wing walking,' he quipped. The effect on his body just seeing her excitement was surreal. His arms ached to wrap around her. His mouth itched to kiss her. His…

'Of course it's horse riding. Idiot.' She threw him an eager yet faux-frustrated look, unclipped her seat belt and was out of the car before he'd turned the engine off. 'Thank you so much. I can't wait.'

He followed her across the gravel path to the stables. 'You said you used to do it so I hope it's a good idea.'

'The best.' She turned and looked a little discombobulated. 'I said I used to do a lot of things.'

'To be fair, yoga and knitting were a bit of a reach for me,' he admitted, finally giving in to temptation and slipping his hand into hers. And slightly regretting that he'd brought her here, and not suggested just cooking her breakfast at his place. Then eating it in bed. Eating her in bed.

'Hey, girl. Hey.' She cooed towards one of the horses. 'Oh, it's been such a long time since I rode a horse. I've been promising myself to book in some sessions but never get round to it. I've never thought about it for a…date.' She looked up at him and her easy smile wavered.

He saw the hesitation and he wondered, too, exactly what this was. Other than hopefully a prelude to more great sex, it was about getting to know each other, right? For their little charade. Not a date. They weren't dating. Even though this felt a lot like a date. 'I thought it would be good to get out and do something rather than just be in a restaurant again. I'm not good at sitting and chatting. I prefer to be active.'

'Me too.' The smile was reminiscent of her post-sex grin the other night and his body prickled in response.

'Lucas!' His old friend George and George's husband, Ivan, wandered out from the stables, arms outstretched in greeting. 'You made it.'

'Hey, guys. How's things?' Lucas shook hands with Ivan, while mentally forcing the tingling sensation to dissipate. 'Ivan, George, this is Ivy.'

'So pleased to meet you.' George shook Ivy's hand then wrapped Lucas in a hug, whispering, 'You sly old dog. This is very unlike you.'

'I know. But don't read anything into it.' He glanced over to Ivy, who was now wandering back to the horses with Ivan.

But George was not going to let him off the hook. 'Oh? That makes me very suspicious. I want all the details while she's being distracted.'

Lucas sighed, not knowing what to say. 'It's a long story.'

George looked at Ivy then back at Lucas. 'You have about two minutes. Be quick.'

'Seriously, have you been talking to my mother?' Lucas laughed. Their friendship had been initiated at a baby swim class both their mothers had attended at the local private gym, then cemented at school. He'd been honoured when George had asked him to be best man around four years ago. That wedding had been a huge surprise because George had always insisted he wasn't the settling-down type, like Lucas. But it was amazing to see how happy he was with Ivan. How one person could make such a difference. At least, for George. Lucas almost envied them…the way they finished each other's sentences, the knowledge that they were loved, cared for. That there was someone to share both adventures and the mundane. Just having each other.

Almost envied him because, for Lucas, it was better for all concerned if he remained uncommitted for the rest of his days. That way, no one got hurt.

'No mothers have been involved, I promise.' George grimaced, because their parents not only shared the same postcode, they also had similar values and expectations. 'I just hate to think of you sad and old and alone.'

'Geez, mate.' Lucas snorted. 'Cheers for the brutal precis of my life.'

'Brutal but true.' George shrugged but slapped him on the back. After forty-plus years' friendship, smack talk was their MO. 'But she seems nice, so I'm not sure what she's doing with you.'

He followed George's line of vision towards Ivy. She had her back to them and was laughing at something Ivan was saying and simultaneously stroking the horse. Her head was tipped back, her slender throat moving as she laughed. Her hair was shimmering different shades of bronze and gold in the sunlight. Her backside was like a peach in black skinny jeans. She was the total package. Beautiful. Funny. Caring. Sexy. His chest suddenly filled with warmth, as if the sun was shining right on him and not on her hair.

He wanted to strip those jeans from her. Lay her down…yes, even on some hay if that was where they were at, and slide inside her.

Ah. That was it.

That was what this weird feeling was. This attraction was entirely physical. He just hadn't had enough sex with her.

Well, that was an easy remedy.

He realised he was probably drooling so drew his gaze back to his old friend. 'Thanks for the loan of the horses. I owe you, big time.'

'Yes, you do. Maybe dinner some time? We can get better acquainted with Ivy.'

'Yeah, well…maybe.' Lucas didn't want to explain, but the thought of lying to his friends as well as his family didn't sit well with him. 'We're really just friends. It's nothing…permanent.'

'Sure it isn't. I've never known you have a girlfriend for longer than two minutes.' George's eyebrows rose as he grilled Lucas. 'You do know you're allowed to trust other people? Not everyone's out to get you.'

Oh, yeah. How had he known George would push him to this? Because it was what he did: dug deep for Lucas's truth. And Lucas knew he wouldn't be fobbed off. 'Trusting Ivy isn't the problem. It's trusting myself.'

His friend frowned. 'For what?'

'You know what.' Lucas knew his voice was almost a mumble now as the memory of what happened all those years ago shot through him like a knife. 'Keeping her safe. Keeping anyone safe.'

'Man, Lucas. If you're talking about what happened with Flora, then you have to forgive yourself.'

'I can't and I won't.' Lucas kept his voice low. 'Seriously. This is just a bit of a laugh. Nothing deep.' But the knife twisted a little more.

'And yet you want to borrow my horses to impress her.'

'I'm not trying to impress her. I just…' he was all out of words with how to describe why he'd suddenly decided to bring her horse riding just because he knew she liked doing it '…thought it would be a fun thing to do.'

George's eyebrows rose and he clearly didn't believe a word. 'I hope she can ride.'

Yes, she can, mate. Very well indeed.

He thought about her catching his rhythm. Or had he caught hers? They'd both been so in tune with each other, had known instinctively what the other wanted and needed. It had been wild and intense and he'd lost himself in her. He couldn't remember semantics. Just how she'd tasted. How she'd felt wrapped around him.

And how doing it again was top of his to-do list, despite all his talk about not committing. But, hell, this was sex, not marriage.

Ivy called over, 'Oh, it's been a while but I'm sure it'll come back to me. I'm itching to get going.'

Lucas wondered exactly how much of the conversation she'd heard but she laughed and looked over at him. 'I hope you can ride too, Lucas.'

'Oh, yes.' He caught her eye, making sure she understood the full innuendo, and she pressed her lips together, bugging her eyes at him to shut up. But he didn't miss the glitter and the heat there too.

She held her hand up to one of the horses, who gave it a good sniff. She stroked its muzzle.

'Aren't you beautiful?' She turned to Lucas and shook her head, her eyes full of tease. 'Just so you don't misunderstand, I was talking to the horse.'

'I wouldn't assume anything else.' But he had to admit he kind of liked the fact that she associated beautiful with him in any kind of way.

He handed her a helmet and then helped fasten it under her chin. The way she looked up at him as he clipped the straps in place, so close, so excited and trusting him to make her helmet safe. That mouth inches away.

It felt natural to press his lips against hers and kiss her.

But he didn't. He held back. Pulled back. Not wanting George to witness any of this and have him doubling down on his questions.

Grinning at them both, George handed him a small backpack. 'Here's a few snacks. There's a great picnic spot down by the marina. You can let the horses rest there a while too. Have fun.'

Lucas's gaze fixed on Ivy again as she put one foot in the stirrup and hoisted herself on top of her horse. She looked majestic up there, powerful like a warrior queen. Once again he thought about stripping her naked and harnessing that power for some serious lovemaking. 'Oh, don't worry. I intend to have fun. Lots.'

Ivy's heart thrilled as they trotted along an undulating path, first through George and Ivan's beautiful farmland, then deep into the native bush park. The air was alive with birdsong, such different sounds from the traffic and bustling street ones she heard from her apartment.

She stroked her horse Patty's neck. 'It's so good to be in the saddle again and breathing in this amazing fresh air after being in the city for so long.'

'Yes.' The path was just wide enough for them to trot side by side. Lucas turned to her and smiled. 'Stuck in the hospital with the air con and disinfectant smell. I'm glad you're enjoying it.'

'Switching off devices and just being in nature is very good for the soul.' She breathed in the cool crisp wintry air. 'I really should do this more often.'

Lucas was very good for the soul too. He looked great there on his horse, relaxed and yet strong. Confident in his physicality and his control of the animal. Lit by the dappled morning light, he looked beautiful and commanding and yet somehow relieved that she was enjoying herself. Just how much thought and effort had he put into this? Had he been anxious it would be a success?

Her heart did a lot more thrilling at this thought. He'd organised this all. For her. Because she said she used to enjoy it. But truth was she wasn't sure what to make of it all. Oh, she knew this was just a bit of fun for them to get to know each other better, but they could have done that in any cafe anywhere in the city. To bring her out here into the countryside, meeting his friends…meant something more. Something deeply personal.

Which made her want to simultaneously wish this perfect morning could last for ever, and also run far away to where the connections they were forming wouldn't get any stronger. Because it was getting harder to ignore the way her body felt when he was around. Not just turned on, but the way her heart smiled.

But if she was going to fulfil her part of the deal, she needed to know more about him so horse riding or coffees or sex…it was all just research. Right?

The path took them to a shallow, narrow, slow-moving creek. The horses stopped and drank the cool, clear water.

'So how do you know George?' Ivy asked him. Watching the way he'd chatted to his friend had intrigued her. They'd been in cahoots about something, heads close together, clearly trying not to be overheard.

Lucas patted his horse's shoulder. 'We go way back. His parents and my parents are friends. We grew up in the same neighbourhood and went to the same schools. He's like another brother to me, really. One who actually tolerates me.'

He gave a wry laugh. 'He'll be at the ball too, with Ivan.'

'Great. Someone I'll actually know.' She hadn't missed the brother comment.

'I think you'll know plenty. Lots of the hospital bigwigs go. The Sydney medical scene is quite incestuous.'

'Tell me about it.' Her thoughts swung to Grant. He'd never have organised a horse-riding trip for her.

But she knew better than to compare. The two relationships were entirely different.

This one was bogus, for a start.

She focused back on Lucas, who was looking at her with a funny expression she couldn't read, reminding her that she didn't know enough about him to know his moods. And, bogus or not, there was something about him that made her want to know more. To understand him more deeply, in a way that probably wasn't going to be good for her in the end.

'Everything okay?' she asked him.

He blinked and snagged her gaze. 'Just thinking about the other night.'

'Oh?' Her body heated in immediate response. He'd been so close a few minutes ago and she'd ached to kiss him, but hadn't because George had been watching and also because they hadn't overtly stated that making out would be on the menu every time they met. 'What about it?'

'I didn't want to lie to George about our deal. I didn't mention it, but I did say we weren't serious. Now I'm wondering if I should have made more of a thing about it in case he mentions anything to his mum. Or mine.'

It was interesting to her that he cared so deeply about people: his friends and his patients. But was so offhand about his family. What was going on there? What had happened? Or was *undemonstrative* just the family dynamic?

He seemed to keep them at arm's length, but was still attending their ball. Was that out of duty? Hell, she knew all about that. Duty had been the Hursts' catch cry growing up. Yet she'd gone against that, against her parents' plans for her. And now her family kept her at arm's length.

Go figure.

'Do we really need to be so analytical about our relationship? We can say things got serious enough for more dates, hence the ball. Then we just...you know...lost interest.' She wondered how quickly she'd lose interest in Lucas and stop trying to work him out. After this 'date'? The next? After their next lovemaking? The time after that?

He nodded. 'You're probably right. Things can get intense and then wither, right? It's not always a straight path from dating to engagement and beyond.'

'Wither?' She laughed as her eyes darted to his trousers.

He sat up straighter in the saddle, chest puffed out. 'No chance of that happening here.'

'Yeah, right.' Giggling, she threw down the verbal gauntlet.

His eyes glittered and his smile was loaded with promise. 'If I wasn't on this horse, Ivy Hurst, I'd show you exactly what I mean.'

'You'd have to catch me first.' She tugged on the reins then squeezed her legs softly into Patty's flank and encouraged her to start off again, leaving Lucas in her dust. Putting space between them while she tried to deal with the way her heart danced at his words and the way her name on his lips made her chest heat and stole the breath from her lungs.

He caught her up quickly and reached out to touch her arm. Sparks of electricity fired across her skin. She inhaled in surprise. This wasn't good for her, all this *feeling*. Her skin, her heart, her chest. She didn't know what to do with it all.

She drew her arm away. Then immediately regretted it because every nerve, every cell in her body craved his touch.

They rode across to the other side of the creek and up a slight incline, past some interesting rock formations and overhangs revealing dark caves, offering what Ivy imagined would be a welcome shade in the height of summer. Then on to a path in a clearing that took them down to Cowan Creek, the main tributary that led eventually to the sea. A few hundred metres further down to the right was a marina and picnic tables, a couple of motorboats, some kayakers and tourists enjoying the winter sunshine. But here it was secluded and private.

Lucas slowed up and looked around. 'Hungry?'

'Starving.'

'Here's good, then. We can sit down on the riverbank in the sunshine.' He slid off his horse and secured the reins around a thick tree trunk with some rope in the backpack George had given them. Then he helped Ivy slip down from Patty, holding her close as she slid down, her body connecting with his at hip, belly, breasts. She clung onto his shoulders, her mouth a hair's breadth from his.

Delicious anticipation made her belly tighten.

He grinned. 'Seems I managed to catch you. In the end.'

'Seems you did.' Her body prickled at the greedy look in his eyes as his gaze roamed down her body as her feet touched the ground.

'You're very good at this.'

She smiled. 'Bit rusty, to be honest. But Patty's very tolerant.'

'I wasn't talking about horse riding.' He clicked his tongue and grabbed Patty's reins.

Took a couple of seconds to secure her next to his horse, Hatty.

The heat of his body lingered on her skin. She was acutely aware of his every movement, every action. The way his hands worked to tie the reins up, how he fussed gently over the horses. His purposeful stride back to her. It was as if they were the only people in the world. As if everything else were less in focus. Less bright. Dimmed.

I'd show you exactly what I mean.

The anticipation tingled through her.

This feeling, these feelings…surely she could cope with them, wrangle them into a box in her heart and close the lid. She wasn't overwhelmed by them. She wouldn't allow herself to be. She wasn't a lustful teenager any more, or even a confused thirty-something trying to make sense of everything. Hell, she was a very experienced nearly forty-year-old; she wasn't about to start losing control over a man.

But for now…why the hell not?

CHAPTER SEVEN

SHE HELD HER breath as he reached out and cupped her cheek. Surprised by the serious way he looked at her, as if searching for an anchor, a lifeline. Then the softening of his gaze as his eyes met hers. As if he'd found it.

His lips touched hers and feverish need swelled through her.

This kiss was filled with all the bundled-up aching of the last few days, the secret smiles, the fleeting eye contact on the ward, in the hospital corridors. The promise.

She wove her arms around his neck as he backed her up against a tree, slipping his leg in between hers. She closed her eyes and pressed against the thick hard line of his erection. Wanting him deep inside her.

She moaned as his tongue slipped into her mouth and the kiss deepened, changing rhythm from slow and intense to heightened and wild. Flashing from a spark to a flame.

He played with the buttons on her denim

jacket. Slipped his hands up under her sweater and cupped her breast over her bra. 'God, Ivy. I've been dreaming about doing this for five days. Every time I see you at work, I want to steal you away and explore your body.'

You too?

Thoughts of him doing this to her had driven her almost crazy over the last few days. He'd infiltrated her dreams and walked through her waking moments like a tantalising treat just out of reach. Every thought had stoked the need to touch him, taste him again.

Her head braced against the tree as she leaned back to look at his face. Her voice was raspy, her breath coming in short gasps as he stroked her tightening nipple through the lace. 'One sure way to get the sack.'

'Worth it, though.' He chuckled against her throat as he tugged her sweater neck down and kissed a trail across her collarbone. 'For this.'

'Really?' Her hands slid between their thighs and down his length and he groaned.

'Well, no, probably not. But almost.' He captured her mouth again. 'Actually. Yes. For more of this.'

The sound of children's laughter getting closer had him peeling himself away from her. 'Damn. Probably need to save the rest for later.'

'Yes.' She tugged her clothes back into position, her brain a fog that had barely registered they were in a public place. 'Later sounds good.'

He kissed her neck. 'Promise?'

'Try and stop me.' She shivered with desire and if it hadn't been for the precious horse riding that he'd arranged for her, she'd have suggested they go straight back to the city now, or that they find a hotel en route. But this had at least answered one question: this was where things stood between them. Desire. Lust. Need. And it made her feel the most alive she'd felt for years. 'Now, about the food…?'

'Sure, thing. Woman cannot live on sex alone, right? Let's see what pleasures Georgie boy has prepared for us.' He opened the rucksack and pulled out a picnic rug, which he flipped onto the grass, then emptied the rest of the contents of the bag onto it. A bottle of sparkling wine, cheese and crackers. Dates, grapes, apples. Cherry tomatoes. Melamine plates, picnic glasses and cutlery.

A small family group sauntered past along the path a few metres from their picnic spot. Lucas waved. Ivy followed suit, then settled back in the warm sunshine, immensely grateful that the children's excited laughter had put a stop to the making out. It seemed that whenever she was around Lucas she was too easily led into temptation.

He dug deeper into the bag. 'Seems George has catered for everything. What's this at the bottom?' He pulled out a small box and grimaced. 'Condoms.'

Ivy chuckled. 'Be prepared, right?'

'George was never a Boy Scout, trust me. He was never that well behaved.' He stuffed them back into the bag. 'I'll have a word. He shouldn't have. I'm sorry.'

'No. Don't. Unless it's to thank him for the laughs. It's funny. And he's right. Got to be safe.'

He shook his head but managed a rueful smile. 'I'll kill him.'

They ate and chatted some more about George and friendships in general. Ivy told him about some of the scrapes she, Harper, Phoebe and Ali had got into over the years and the tight friendship they all had again now that Ali and Harper's rift was healed. 'Honestly, I don't know how I'd have got through my split from Grant without them. You know who your true friends are when you hit hard times, right?'

He nodded. 'I don't know them well, only as colleagues. But they seem like good people.'

'They really are. And now we're all back at the same hospital. Such fun.'

'Not the same kind of fun that I imagine when I see you across a crowded ER.' His pupils flared with heat. But then he said, 'Hey, actually, I know we probably shouldn't be talking about work but…'

'Well, why not? It's what connects us, after all.'

'Is it? Not the amazing sex? Out-of-this-world kisses? Our dodgy, daring deal?' He bugged his eyes at her and handed her some earthy Camembert on a cracker.

'You know what I mean.' She threw him a shady frown. 'Work is pretty much ninety per cent of my life so I'm happy to have a quick conversational diversion there if you want.'

'Okay. So, how's Emma doing post-surgery? I mean, I've seen the charts and chatted to her so I know physically she's doing well, but emotionally?'

'Emotionally?'

Interesting.

'She's good, actually. I think that as long as the babies are growing and developing, she's fine. She's obviously still very sore after yet another surgery, but happy to have one less thing to worry about. And an appendix removal was an easy fix, even though I'm worried about the amount of anaesthetic she and the babies are having.'

'I know. But I need to clean up some of those grafts. I want to get her healed and home and dealing with the scar management asap. If you think she's up to it all.'

'I do. She's been through a lot but she's a very strong woman. I'm happy for you to start on Monday. That way we can have her used to the protocol before her brain is filled up with baby delivery, feeding and everything else a new mum has to deal with.'

'Okay.' He blew out a deep breath. 'That's great. Brilliant.'

Something about his questioning over the last few weeks, though, had been niggling her. 'Okay, so what's going on with her?'

'What do you mean?' He blinked. Clearly confused. Rattled almost. And she immediately regretted steering the conversation into this territory. But she'd started now and she wanted to fill in some of the gaps of her understanding of how he ticked.

'I don't know. I see the way you deal with her, like treating her burns is...personal somehow.'

'I just want to do my best for her. Like all my patients.' He leaned away and frowned. The light in his eyes had dimmed and his posture was tight. He'd backed off emotionally and she wondered if she'd pressed too hard.

'Sorry, I don't want to make things sound weird. We all came into medicine to help people. Why did you choose to be a reconstructive surgeon? Was it the family thing?'

'What do you mean? Family...?' For the slightest moment he looked panic-stricken. His mouth formed a thin line, his shoulders rose and his eyes darted away. His reaction was oddly guarded.

'Their plastic surgery clinic,' she emphasised.

When he looked back at her there was a sort

of forced jollity to his tone. 'Yes, of course. The clinic. I never wanted to work there, to be honest. Not that there's anything wrong with appearance medicine, it's just not my bag. I can do more good working for the public sector, helping those who can't afford it but really need it. And I like to see the treatment through from emergency admission to discharge.'

'All your family work there except you. Brothers and sister?'

'Yes. All happy to join the family firm. Flora's not a doctor, though. She was…' His eyes darkened. 'Well, she works in the administration department.'

What a strange reaction to her inane question. There was more to this family thing, she knew. He just wasn't going to elaborate.

Which intrigued her and niggled too, because, after everything they'd already done and his promise and clear desire to share more, he still couldn't trust her with his innermost thoughts.

It's just fun, she reminded herself.

They weren't soulmates. She didn't need to know everything about him. But she wanted to. And that was probably the biggest warning that she needed to stay away from him.

It was starting to dawn on her that her heart was at risk here. Because even though alarm bells were chiming, she just couldn't get enough of him.

* * *

Ivy had steered the conversation a little too close for Lucas's comfort. He wasn't ready to talk about Flora or why he stayed away from his family. It wasn't just because of his meddling mother, but because he simply didn't fit there. Every moment with them reminded him of that terrible day. Every look they gave him, he was sure, was imbued with blame.

He didn't know if he'd ever be ready to admit to Ivy what he'd done. That was something he never shared and only his closest friends from that time knew what had happened. Why bring it all up and ruin a good day?

The smell of grilled meat wafted towards them and he looked over to the picnic area down the shoreline to see four young guys—mid to late teens—standing at one of the barbecues.

After he'd skirted the conversation Ivy had seemingly taken it as ended so she picked up the plates and cutlery and was rinsing them in the river to clean them until they could wash them properly back at George's place. She looked over at the young men and raised her eyebrows. 'They look like they're having a good time.'

He watched the guys now chasing each other, play-fighting with kayak paddles, whooping and messing round.

'God, remember those carefree days?' He

wandered over to the horses and gave them an apple each. 'In my head I'm still twenty-three.'

She laughed. 'Gosh, no, thanks. I don't want to live through that time again. All that angst and trying to impress people, working out who you are. I like knowing exactly who I am and what I want.'

After dealing with the horses, making sure they were happy and comfortable, he wandered back to stand next to her. 'Which is what? Who are you, Ivy?'

She turned to him, eyes bright and focused. He had no doubt she knew exactly who she was and what she wanted. 'I'm a good doctor advancing well in my career. I'm a great mentor and grab teaching moments whenever appropriate. I'm a good friend, but I'd like to be a better one. I miss things every now and then because I work late.'

'Miss what kind of things?'

The young men's laughter wafted towards them. They'd finished eating and were now climbing into kayaks. None of them wore a life vest. She turned back to watch them. 'I missed that Harper and Yarran have moved in together and goodness knows what else. I'd like to be more a part of their lives.'

'I'm sure they understand. Doctors have a hard job, we work late and long hours.'

She shook her head. 'That's not a good enough excuse. We're all doctors. I'm trying to be better.'

'I get it. With George out here in the Woop Woops and me living in the city I don't get to see him nearly often enough.' He watched as she smiled in agreement, the way the dappled light made her skin all shadows and light.

He knew all about the light, he'd breathed it in when he'd slid inside her and had seen the shadows in her eyes as she'd talked about her break-up, but he didn't know much else about her. Hungry for more insight into her life, he asked, 'What about your family? You don't talk about them much.'

'Not a lot to say.' She looked out at the water, wrapped her arms around her chest.

He gently pushed to find out more. 'How many siblings?'

'One brother, one sister. I'm in the middle. Which probably explains a lot.' She rolled her eyes. 'The trouble-causing, rabble-rousing middle child.'

'Bring on the rabble-rousing. It sounds interesting.' When she didn't elucidate on any previous rabbles, he said, 'You said you grew up in an army family.'

She turned to him, looking surprised. 'I'm impressed you remembered. Yes. We moved around a lot from one army base to another.'

'Must have been difficult to make friends if you were always on the go.'

She sighed. 'We had each other, I guess. But I was very happy when I came here to med school and met Phoebe, Ali and Harper. They became my surrogate family.'

'You weren't close to your real one any more?'

Her mouth formed a straight line. 'We had a falling-out.'

'You too?' But he couldn't imagine she'd done anything as bad as he had to cause the fall-out.

She sighed deeply and raised her eyebrows. 'The Hursts have a strong military tradition and they expected each of us to follow in their footsteps.'

'And you didn't want to?'

She shook her head. 'Not likely. I wanted to be a doctor from the moment I knew what one was. Earlier, probably.'

'You could have been a doctor in the army—'

He glanced up as the sound of a boat engine roared through the congenial bush sounds. A motorboat was traveling at speed. Lucas gulped. 'Whoa. He's going fast.'

Ivy nodded, pale now and watching intensely. 'And heading straight towards the kayakers.'

'Oh, God.' Lucas ran to the shoreline and saw the trajectory the boat was on. The kayakers were playing some sort of game that involved hitting the water hard with their paddles and showering each other in plumes of spray. One was standing in his kayak, arms wide, singing at the top of his voice. The others were whooping and laughing and had music playing from a boom box so loud Lucas could hear it from the shoreline. None of them were paying any attention to anything else on the river. None of them had noticed the boat careening towards them.

Lucas shouted at the boat. 'Hey! Slow down. Kayakers!' He turned to Ivy, hoping she wasn't going to witness something tragic… He could see the inevitable unfolding of events and could barely look himself. 'He shouldn't be going that fast. Is he even looking where he's going?'

'Stop! Slow down!' Ivy shouted, waving her arms frantically in the air. 'Stop!'

But it happened before anyone could have stopped it. Three of the kayakers had somehow noticed and managed to get out of the way, but the one that had been standing up was still in direct line of the boat, now frantically paddling and making no significant headway away. The boat skipper appeared to see him just in time, steered the boat sharply right, but caught the side of the kayak.

It was difficult to see through the wash of the water but, when the boat had cleared and the swell calmed, the kayak was empty.

'Hell. Where is he?' Lucas scanned the water.

One of the kayakers had dived into the water.

One was pointing into the river. One was hurling abuse at the boat skipper, who had quieted the engine.

'Phone for an ambulance. And the police. And stay here.' Lucas stripped off his top and jeans and waded waist deep into the freezing water, then dived under. When he surfaced he tried to catch his breath. It was so cold. Too cold. And none of them had life jackets.

He thrashed across the water towards the huddle of kayakers. Just as he reached them one of them surfaced, dragging the dunked kayaker with him. Blood was streaming from the injured man's nose and his cheek looked misshapen and lumpy.

'Get him up here.' Lucas helped lift the injured kayaker out and up onto the front of one of the kayaks. 'What's his name?'

'Sione,' his friend said.

'Sione, hi. My name is Lucas and I'm a doctor. Can you tell me where it hurts?'

'Here,' the guy croaked, holding his right hand up to his face, 'and here.' He pointed to his left biceps, where more blood streamed from a deep, thick gash.

Thank goodness he was breathing and moving all limbs. It could have been a whole lot worse. Lucas steadied himself on the rocking kayak. 'Okay. Let's take a look at the damage.'

He was just finishing assessing Sione's facial injuries when Ivy popped up out of the water. Her lips were blue, her face a ghostly white. He shook his head. She shouldn't be here in icy swirling water. What if something happened to her too? 'What the hell are you doing here? It's freezing.'

'Yes, it is.' She hauled herself up onto one of the other kayaks in just her bra and panties and stared at him. 'Thought you might need an extra pair of medical hands. Ambulance is on its way. ETA about five minutes. Luckily, there was one in the neighbourhood.'

Lucas grimaced at the clumsy way he'd spoken to her. He'd underestimated her. Or rather, had wanted to protect her from seeing this, being involved in this, getting wet. Getting cold. But he'd ignored the fact that she was a doctor and would want to help as much as he would. 'Looks like a broken nose and possibly fractured cheek. And a nasty gash on his biceps.'

The water was deceptively choppy and made it difficult to tend to the guy's injuries. They had nothing to stem the bleeding other than what little clothing they wore. Ivy crooked her finger at the boat skipper, who'd at least had the good grace to come back and help. 'Throw us a towel. Something, anything to stem the bleeding.'

Red-faced, the man threw a white fluffy towel.

'I'm sorry. I really am. Can I take him back to shore?'

'No way am I getting on that boat.' Sione shook his head sharply.

'Sione, honestly, it's the best way to get you warm and administer proper care.' Ivy held onto the one-person kayak as it rocked. She was cramped up, sitting on the deck with one of the other kayakers—some scrawny youth, with a smattering of facial hair that was pretending to be a beard, in the seat—and at risk of capsizing.

'No way. I should sue him.' Sione's lips were dark and his face pale with shock.

'Okay. We're wasting time here arguing and we're all going to get hypothermia on top of everything else.' Lucas nodded. 'I'll kayak you over. I think this is just about seaworthy.' He examined the side of the damaged kayak. There was a good deal of scraped and scratched fibreglass but it was not letting in water. 'Won't take long.'

The kid with the beard looked at Ivy, appraising her in her underwear. His lascivious smile said it all. 'You can definitely come with me.'

'Thanks. I appreciate that.' Ivy shuffled back a little and held on.

Lucas started to paddle, his annoyance fuelling his strokes. He did not like the way beard guy—beard *kid*—was looking at Ivy, even if she did look amazing, all perfect curves and slim legs. She was not for general consumption.

He did not like that she'd got wet and cold.

He did not like the twist in his chest at the thought of her being in any kind of danger. At all. Not when she was with him.

And he definitely didn't like all these emotions welling up in him. Over a…friend.

'Here we go.' Lucas helped Sione onto the jetty, secured the kayak on the shore then looked around for something to warm his patient up.

The other two kayaks hit the shoreline and Ivy jumped off, shouting to the other kayakers, 'Go grab your clothes and towels and come straight back. We've got to warm Sione up.'

She was clearly on exactly the same wavelength.

'You want me to grab your stuff too?' beard guy asked as his eyes hungrily skimmed down Ivy's body.

She didn't seem to notice. 'Great. Thanks. It's over there in the clearing. Just bring our clothes, please, and make sure the horses are okay.'

'Gotcha.'

'Be quick. She's…' Lucas corrected himself even though his intention was getting Ivy warm. She was shivering so forcefully her legs were literally shaking. And then there was Sione to look after. '*We're* freezing.'

He threw beard kid an icy look. Stifling the

urge to say something more was almost killing him, but he knew Ivy would be furious if he went all macho and protective on her. Theirs was not that kind of relationship.

But it didn't stop him wanting to throw the kid in the river just for looking at her.

The sound of an engine being cut had Lucas looking up. The motorboat skipper was running over to them. 'Mate. Seriously, are you okay?'

Lucas had held back while he assessed Sione but irritation now flowed out of him, probably fuelled by beard guy too, if he was honest. 'You could have killed him. What the hell were you doing?'

'I was sorting out the water-ski rope.' The man shook his head and looked at his feet. 'I didn't see them.'

'That was obvious.'

He knelt next to Sione and handed him another towel. 'I'm sorry, mate.'

'I'm not your mate.' Sione held the towel to his nose, the white towelling slowly taking on a pink tinge. 'Like I said before, I should sue you.'

'Hey, who was the one messing around on the water?' the skipper threw back.

Lucas stood. 'We have enough witnesses who saw your carelessness. You were going too fast, not looking where you were going. It could have been a lot more serious. The police are on their way.' He ignored the man's huffing and turned to Sione. 'Give me that towel and I'll press it on your arm wound to try to stop the bleeding. You're making a mess of the jetty.' He threw him a smile just to soften the mood.

'Give it here, I'll do that. You hold the other towel to his face.' Ivy knelt down next to them. 'I wish I had my doctor's bag with me. I've got painkillers in there that would definitely help.'

Lucas nodded, trying to focus on Sione's injuries and not on the swell of Ivy's breasts in that white lacy bra. The frill of skimpy panties that caressed her backside. Her soft, smooth skin. She'd scraped her wet hair back off her face and she looked radiant, athletic. He remembered the press of her thighs as she rocked in rhythm with him. She was so damned hot.

And shivering with cold.

Beard kid turned up with their stuff at the same time the ambulance arrived. Within minutes everyone was warmed up either from their dry clothes, silver foil-blankets or hot chocolate from the nearby cafe. The cafe owner had come out to see what all the fuss had been about and returned with a tray of steaming drinks and biscuits.

By now the police had arrived too and were taking statements from everyone.

'Will I get into trouble?' Sione whispered to Lucas.

'For what? Having fun? As far as I'm aware there's no law against that.'

'I wasn't…concentrating. We were just having a laugh. My mum always tells me I'm too much of a clown and that I have to be more responsible.' Sione hung his head. 'And now there's the ambulance call-out fee to pay too. I'm so lame.'

Lucas's heart went out to him. How many times had he called himself worse names than that? How many nights had he lain awake wishing he could rewind time and make better decisions? And he'd been a lot younger than Sione here. 'You are not lame, Sione. That boat skipper should have been paying more attention. He was going far too fast and not watching where he was headed.'

'Yeah, but we should have been watching too.'

'True. But you weren't going to cause any real harm by messing about. Not like him. I doubt the police will have any cause to charge you. But for the record: wear a life jacket next time and pay attention.'

'Yes. Will do.' Sione stepped up into the ambulance. 'Thanks.'

'Oh, and give me a call if you have any trouble with that wound. It's nasty.' He gave Sione his number. 'I'm a burns and plastics surgeon, so I can help down the track if you need me to.'

'Yeah, man. Thanks again.'

A gentle nudge in his ribs had Lucas turning

to see Ivy at his side. She winked at him. 'That was really nice of you.'

'Yeah. I'm like that.' He shrugged, feigning nonchalance but feeling a heat of pride under her gaze.

'Seriously, you didn't have to offer to help him. You've done enough already.'

'If I can help him, I will. He's just a kid.'

But the tumble in his chest as he watched the paramedics lead Sione to the ambulance wasn't nice at all. He remembered those feelings of shame and regret all too well. Stupid choices made by an immature kid. The physical hurt had meant little to him, but the emotional pain lingered to this day, like a brand on his heart that would be there for ever.

Ivy slipped her arm into his. 'We'd better get Patty and Hatty. They'll be missing us.'

'Sure.' Her presence was reassuring and anchoring. He wanted to wrap his arms around her, feel her heart beating against his. Breathe in her scent and hold her close. Not just because she was soft and warm and so damned sexy, but because he knew he'd feel better there. With her.

Which was crazy.

She turned to look up at him, her gaze soft and light. Her smile genuine. 'Are you okay, Lucas?'

He nodded, unable to answer in words. Because if he thought that someone else could erase his pain, he was a fool. No one ever had before.

And more, he didn't deserve to have it erased anyway.

And yet, there was something about Ivy…her smile, her belief in him, her trust…that gave him hope for the first time in many years.

So, he wasn't sure he was okay at all.

CHAPTER EIGHT

LUCAS WAS QUIET all the way back to the city and Ivy wasn't sure why. Something had bothered him earlier and she couldn't put her finger on what. He'd been in superhero mode when he'd dived into the river to save Sione, but then later he'd shut down.

Oh, he still made conversation, and made sure she was warm and comfortable, and had been almost jolly with George and Ivan as if he'd made a real effort to seem cheerful, but it was as if his fire had gone out. She didn't think she'd said or done anything wrong, so she knew it wasn't about her. But he just seemed…troubled.

So when he invited her up to his apartment for a takeaway dinner she accepted. Just so she could dig a little deeper and unlock some of the things he wasn't telling her. Because she needed to know enough about him in case his parents referred to some shared family memory or joke from the past that was significant. Or in case he was just a moody old boot and they mentioned that too. So she could agree and laugh it off or defend him or…whatever. And to be able to describe his apartment if his mother asked.

And she wanted to see where he lived, and… if she was being totally honest with herself…to be with him a little longer, quiet or loud or anything in between.

'I think I'm going to get vertigo if this takes us up any higher.' She looked out of the elevator window as the buildings and trees grew smaller and smaller, and then there was nothing but a concrete wall to look at as they shot skywards.

'You get used to it. Hold onto me if you want.' He grinned, offering his arm, and for a few moments she had her old Lucas back. But he didn't make any kind of move on her as she'd thought he might. Hadn't pressed her against the elevator wall as he had against the tree.

The lift jolted to a halt and the doors opened. He stepped out and beckoned her forward. 'Here we go.'

'Wow! Just wow.' She stepped into his place and her breath was sucked out of her lungs. From this vantage point she could see the Sydney harbour bridge and endless ocean beyond, but she was distracted by the alabaster decor and black and white marble kitchen bench on the right of the open-plan living space. Truffle-coloured sofas by the window softened the sleek lines of the white lacquered window frames.

It looked homely and comfortable but very, *very* expensive.

She had no idea how much a place like this would cost but she'd bet it was more than she could ever afford. Which highlighted to her even more his wealthy background.

The thought of his parents grounded her to the reality of their situation. The Matthewses were powerful movers in the Sydney medical scene. They probably had influence and friends who ran the Sydney Central hospital. One word from them and her career progression could be suddenly limited, or terminated altogether. So she needed to be careful exactly how much she lied, how dressed up their stories were. Who knew what could be at risk if she messed this up? Or upset them in some way?

He walked her across white floorboards to a floor-to-ceiling window. Outside, the sun was starting to dip, bathing the cirrocumulus clouds and harbour in a rich pinky orange glow. Tiny lights flickered to life in numerous buildings across the bay, like myriad new fireflies twinkling.

Kind of how she felt too when she was with Lucas. As if she'd been cocooned for years and now everything was fresh and bright and new. And, like fireflies' short life span, with a use-by date. A deadline.

She looked out and sighed. 'What an amazing view. I feel like I can see for miles.'

'That's because you can. As soon as I saw this place was being built, I jumped on it. It's the best view in Sydney. I could look at it for hours.' His smile was genuine and his shoulders relaxed. Finally. As if his home gave him sanctuary.

She liked that idea. That he was a homebody too and had his own personal place to unwind as she had. 'Well, I can definitely chat with your mum about this place. There aren't enough words to describe how amazing it is.'

'Sure.' He was still staring out of the window and she had a feeling she'd lost him to his thoughts again.

'Sure?' She drew her gaze away from the window and looked directly at him. 'You've been mightily distracted since Sione. Is something bothering you?'

He blinked and frowned. Then shook his head as if clearing away a thought. 'Ah, really? I'm fine. Just decompressing.'

'Oh, yes. I know that feeling. Sometimes I have so much pent-up adrenalin at the end of a hard day I don't know what to do. Running helps. A long soak. Quiet times.'

'Sorry.' He pulled her close and nuzzled against her head. 'I'm not always good company.'

She leaned her head against his chest and inhaled his scent. It grounded her, the way his embrace did. 'You are excellent company. You arranged for me to go horse riding and I had a fantastic time...apart from watching an almost disaster unfold.' Had that caused this shift in his demeanour? Something to do with the accident? 'I was a bit spooked, to be honest. I really thought that boat was going to do more damage.'

'The water was so cold and choppy. I didn't want you to have to come in. I couldn't deal with you getting into trouble as well.' His eyes narrowed and it occurred to her that this was the same expression she'd seen on his face when she'd popped up out of the water by the kayaks. Fired up. Possessive, almost.

And the fact he'd cared so much about her well-being made her heart squeeze. 'But I was fine. I can swim probably as well as you.'

'Yeah, well. I know that now. I also didn't know you were so damned determined to be part of the rescue team.' His throat made a soft noise, like a chuckle. 'I needn't have worried. You are one capable woman.'

'Seriously, Lucas, you don't have to worry about me at all. You certainly don't have to protect me.' She stroked his cheek, relieved that his reserve had just been worry about keeping her—and no doubt everyone else—safe. 'I can handle myself perfectly well.'

'I can see that. I should have remembered

about the time you tried to kneecap me with a chair on wheels.'

'That's me.' She giggled. 'Rabble-rousing again. But I can be nice too. Light and dark, right?'

Little wisdom lines fanned out at the corners of his eyes as he laughed. 'I was thinking exactly that earlier.'

'What? About me?'

'About the way you're so breezy and helpful…some might call it possessive…' He grinned pointedly at the accusation she'd once thrown at him. 'With your patients. So mindful of your friends and what you want out of life. And it makes me want to do something particularly nasty to Grant for treating you the way he did and dulling your light.'

'Oh, I never told you.' How could she have not mentioned she'd already sealed her part of the deal? 'I bumped into Grant the other day in Perc Up.'

Lucas stepped back, his smile folding. 'And?'

'I don't know. I'm not sure. He was a bit gushy…you can never tell with Grant because he's the world's biggest flirt. But he said I looked great.'

'There you go. Result.' But he tilted his head and looked at her, eyes narrowing. His smile flatlined. 'Does he want you back?'

'Actually, I think he might.' She tried to hide the smile she knew would be just a tad smug.

'We were right about him being jealous when he sees what he's missing.'

Another step back. 'And you? Do you want him back?'

She shuddered at the thought. 'Come on. We're talking about Grant here. There is not a single part of me that wants anything to do with him. Besides, I am not in the habit of kissing one guy when I want to be with someone else.'

He froze, eyes growing wide. 'You want to *be* with me?'

Her heart seemed to stop beating. That wasn't the direction their relationship was going in.

Us. There would be no us.

She remembered their deal. Believed in it too. But the words had shot out before she'd had time to register them. Her brain scrambled to smooth things over.

'I mean… I wouldn't kiss one person then…' She closed her eyes and breathed out deeply. *Rewind.* 'It was just a turn of phrase. I meant I wouldn't be hanging out with two guys at the same time.' She laughed but knew it sounded forced. 'Fine for others to do it if they want, but I barely have the energy for one guy, let alone two.'

'Okay…' He breathed out, but looked as if he was still holding onto some air.

'I don't want to be with Grant. Or anyone…

I'm just enjoying this time. Getting to play a little. I really, really like that.'

'It's just that I don't *be* with anyone.' He grimaced and laughed and the shadows in his face faded away. The atmosphere became lighter again. 'I have no idea what that even means.'

'It's okay. We're definitely on the same page. I'm surprised at myself, but I like you. I like getting to know a bit more about how the other half live. This really is something else.' She drew an arc pointing out the expensive apartment and the ten-million-dollar view. 'And I like the sex.'

Heat flared in his eyes at that. 'Me too.'

'But don't go getting all hung up thinking I'm going to hang around after the ball. I'm not the clingy type.' She thought about her little flat, her own unwinding place. Her sanctuary. She'd spent a long time making it all hers after Grant had moved out. She liked her own space. Not having someone else to clear up after or to take into account. Not having to make conversation when she didn't feel like it. And now she even felt guilty about pushing Lucas to talk when he'd clearly just needed some peace and quiet. 'I don't want to start sharing lives or anything.'

'Right. Good.' He nodded.

'Good.' She didn't know what else to say.

The silence between them stretched but she held his gaze, thinking about how they'd already shared so much just today. She'd learnt so much more about him: that he could ride a horse as well as she did. The fact he'd arranged that for her. She'd met his kind and loving friends who clearly held him in high esteem, had seen him stridently working in an emergency despite taking a risk of his own in freezing water and trying to make Sione feel better and offering further help. Learnt he had quiet times, that he did not hold himself in the same esteem his friends did.

Then sharing his personal place here.

They had a history now. Shared jokes. Whether or not she liked it, or wanted it, their lives were tangling. Not just out of necessity, but because there was this inescapable pull to spend time with him. And she had an inkling he felt it too. There was something more than physical.

Although the physical was *great*.

Her mind flipped to earlier when they'd almost been caught making out. She wanted to rewind them both to that playful moment against the tree rather than this more intense moment neither of them needed.

She let her eyes roam his face.

He watched her too, close enough to play with a lock of her hair, letting it run through his fingers. Every cell in her body ached for the touch of those fingers. Her nipples beaded at the thought.

His gaze was locked on hers. 'Ivy?'

She swallowed, wondering if he was thinking the same thing she was. 'Yes?'

'What exactly are you thinking right now?'

She giggled. 'Why?'

'Because your smile is…blowing my mind.'

'How so?'

'You look like you've just had the best sex of your life.'

'Wishful thinking.' Pressing her lips together, she reached out and touched his hand, curling her fingers around his. Just that moment of skin-on-skin contact sent shock waves of need through her. This was crazy. She touched people all the time—it was her job to touch people when she examined them, when she shook hands, when she comforted—but she never had this tingling, aching need the way she did with Lucas. 'Do you want to revisit that moment back at the tree?'

The growing bulge in his jeans told her he did but he shrugged nonchalantly, as if it would be no big deal. Even though they both knew it was. 'I guess I could be convinced.'

The smile he gave her said he already was.

His mouth was on hers before she took her next breath.

He didn't need asking twice. He pressed his mouth to hers, relishing her taste and tenderness. Yes, tender and soft. Kissing her was intoxicating. Each time was different. Good different.

Mind-blowingly different. Tender. Soft. Wild. Undone. He was never sure which kiss he was going to get, which was the best, which kiss he wanted.

But she always gave him exactly what he needed. It was like mainlining an addictive drug. Dangerous and possibly life-altering, yet there was no way he wanted to—or could—give it up. And he wanted to see her reaction, didn't want to take his eyes away from hers. 'Look at me.'

Her pupils dilated, and a moan escaped her throat. That simple sound arrowed deep in his belly, stoking the desire, making him hot and hard. Hotter and harder.

He cupped her face, fingertips scraping her temples as the kiss deepened. Tongues dancing, exploring. Messy. Wet.

Somehow, he helped her off with her sweater and T-shirt. Wiggled her out of her jeans. She divulged him of his top and jeans too. He kissed her again, not wanting to ever be too far from her mouth, his hands sliding to her bra. It was still damp from the river. Her body prickled with goosebumps and she shivered. She was cold and he'd been too busy freaking out over how connected and intimate they were becoming he hadn't even noticed.

'Right.' He slid his arms under her knees and picked her up.

'What the actual hell are you doing?' She

laughed. 'We're far too old for this. You'll hurt yourself.'

'Not a chance.' He strode through to the bathroom and put her down. 'Time to get you warm.'

He flicked on the shower tap in the large walk-in shower, then stripped her panties and bra off. When the water was the perfect temperature he threw off his boxers, took her hand and led her in.

He positioned her under the flow of water. Laughing, she tipped her head back and let the warm water stream down her slender throat, over her breasts and lower. He stood there, watching her, unable to move.

This was like something from a dream. He felt fifteen again, trying to get a grip on his libido.

And failing.

'You are the most beautiful woman I have ever seen.' He pumped shampoo from a tub and lathered it into bubbles, then massaged it into her hair.

'That feels so good.' Her head lolled back and she looked like something from a painting. Ecstasy on her face, perfection, vulnerability. Soaked. Perfect.

He rinsed the bubbles off then applied conditioner, followed by shower gel. Starting at her neck, he washed her back, then her breasts, flicking her nipples into tight buds that he sucked into his mouth one at a time.

She grasped his hair. 'Oh, Lucas.'

The sensuous slide of the liquid over skin was mesmerising, her body silky soft and smooth.

She pumped liquid soap into her palm and did the same to him. Her fingers slipping and sliding and rubbing over his shoulders, chest, belly. Then she slid her hands over his erection.

'God.' He groaned as she squeezed gently. 'I need to be inside you.'

She kissed her assent, sliding one leg up his thigh, pressing her intimate, soft part against his hardness.

'Here.' He reached over to the cabinet and pulled out a packet of condoms, grabbed a foil, tore it open and was sheathed in less than a minute.

'You have them stashed around the apartment?' She laughed. 'Lucas Matthews. You are a freaking stud.'

He growled. He was only a stud because she was a goddess. 'Bathroom and bedroom. Easy to reach.'

'Good.' She ran her fingertips down his chest and looked up at him. The playful replaced with serious. 'I want you, Lucas. Now.'

He grabbed her leg, hauling it up to his waist, and slid deep inside her, gasping at the feel of heat and wet. She inhaled on a cry.

He froze. He'd hurt her? Typical bloody Lucas. 'Hey, baby. You okay?'

'Better than okay. I just… God, that feels so good.' She rocked with him. 'I'm so hot for you I don't think I can hang on.'

'Then don't.' He gripped her waist and sank deeper into her. Over and over. He wanted to watch her lose control, wanted to take her over the edge. He thrust again and took her mouth with his, kissing her deeply. She moved her hips, angling so he could go deeper and harder.

Then he felt her tighten. And he was lost to the feeling of her orgasm pulsing around him, the soft wetness of her skin, the damp hair that fell over her face as she rocked, the melting hot kisses.

He'd worried he might lose her today in that swirling river. That he wouldn't be able to save her if she'd got into danger. But it had been her who'd saved him. By soft words and understanding. By believing in him. With the gift of her smile and her kisses.

And here she was now in his arms, crying out his name on scraggy breaths as she collapsed against him.

His heart tightened, his chest contracted. He thrust one more time, so deep, so hard and he followed her over that edge.

CHAPTER NINE

SPENT, SATISFIED AND BREATHLESS, he wrapped her in a towel, picked her up again and carried her through to his bed. He lay next to her and stroked her hip, allowing his mind to settle the way his body now had. At least for the moment.

It had been worth every second of the wait since he'd kissed her this morning. But he really, really hoped it wouldn't be that long…almost a whole week…before he was inside her again.

Give him five minutes…

Her eyes flickered open and she glanced over his shoulder to the other side of the room. She gripped his arm. 'Oh, my God, Lucas.'

'What? What is it?' He jumped and twisted and followed her gaze, putting his arm out to protect her. His heart stalled. What the hell?

'Your bookshelves span the entire wall.' She pointed to his huge white bookcase overflowing with books.

His heart started to beat again and he laughed. It seemed his need to protect her overrode everything, including common sense. ‘Geez, woman, I thought there was an intruder. Or a spider. Yes? I have books.’

Her eyes twinkled with excitement. ‘You said you were a beach bum.’

He laughed. ‘*You* said I was a beach bum.’

‘You let me believe it.’

‘You seemed to like the idea of me being all beefcake and a bear of little brain.’ He pulled her closer and whispered, ‘You just want me for my body.’

‘Well…it’s not a bad body… I suppose. But your brain…and books? Delicious.’ Giggling, she slid out of bed, wrapped the top sheet around her…as if he hadn’t just soaped and kissed every inch of her…and wandered over to look at his book collection.

From this vantage point he could see the soft curve of her breast. The little upturned nose. The strident gaze as she perused his collection. His heart contracted. A book lover too. Was there no end to this attraction?

She ran her fingers across the book spines of classics mingled with the latest thrillers. ‘You’ve read all these?’

‘Most of them.’

She grinned and put her hand to her heart. ‘You might just be the perfect man.’

‘I doubt that very much.’

He did not allow his head to swerve back to

that night all those years ago. He refused to allow those memories to intrude on this. He hadn't felt so contented and connected in a long time and he wanted to prolong the moment where someone actually liked him. Where she didn't believe he was the cause of all that hurt…because she didn't know.

And she wouldn't know because he wouldn't tell her. He didn't want to see that sharp intake of breath, the fake smile that she'd have to make to show she wasn't shocked, the insistence that it wasn't his fault. That everything was okay when it wasn't. How could it be okay when his sister still bore the scars?

But, right now, right here, just for once he wanted to forget all that. Because he wanted to make Ivy smile. Keep her smiling. Let her believe he was as good as she thought he was.

She came back to bed with a copy of the latest Amor Towles book and put it on the bedside table. 'I've been wanting to read this for ages. Could I borrow it?'

'Have it. It's excellent. Better, I think, than his last one.'

'No way. I loved *A Gentleman in Moscow*.' She tucked her still-damp hair behind her ear. 'I'll read it and get back to you with a review.'

He chuckled. 'You do that. I'll be interested to hear what you think.' And he really would be. He'd never got this deep and close to a woman where they shared interests like this. Although, that was probably because he'd never given any relationship time to develop.

His fault, he knew. But this was…illuminating.

She poked him in the ribs, making him squirm. 'You're such a dark horse. How many more secrets do you have that I need to find out?'

Too many.

'What you see is what you get. Bear and brawn and…yeah, I guess, a small amount of brain.' He wrapped his arms around her and pulled her to lie down next to him. Because secrets didn't always need to be bad. 'Except…maybe you'll like this… No one except me knows this is even here.'

'What?' She leaned her head against his shoulder, and he inhaled her scent, which, like her touch and her taste, had imprinted on his memory banks.

'If I press this button…see what happens.' The crank of a machine broke through the silence and the shutters above his bed slid apart, bringing a blast of cold air into the room.

Her eyes grew wider as she stared upwards into the darkness. 'Wow. A skylight. The whole ceiling is a skylight?'

'Not all, but…well, most.'

'Oh, my God. This is amazing. I am literally seeing stars.'

He pressed a kiss to her head, enchanted by her excitement. Then he scrambled for his phone on the floor and found the night sky app. 'Apparently there's a whole load of zodiac constellations up there. What's your star sign?'

'You first.' She tilted her head to look at the sky from a different angle.

'Capricorn. There.' He showed her the app and then found it in the night sky. 'It looks like an arrowhead.'

'Oh, yes. I see it. Is that December? January?'

He nodded. 'December the twenty-eighth.'

'Sucks to have your birthday so close to Christmas.' She turned to look at him and pouted.

He copied her expression. 'Indeed it does. Your celebration gets lost in the post-Christmas flop and the pre-New Year excitement.'

'Poor baby.' She slicked a kiss onto his mouth. 'Does that make you feel better?'

'Kind of. Maybe a bit more might help.'

She obliged with a long, silky, wet kiss that had his body tingling with need.

Eventually, she pulled away and sighed. 'My brother's birthday is on January the second and he hates all the shared presents he gets. And he always complains that everyone's still too hungover from New Year's Eve for his birthday party.' Her eyes glittered as she smiled. 'Thank goodness we're talking about birthdays. I'd completely forgotten to even ask you about it. It would seem weird to your mum if I didn't know something that basic about you.'

His mum. The deal. There he'd been, almost convinced this was real. He reminded himself that she was in this to make Grant jealous. That was all…apart from the sex, of course. A little bit of fun. She didn't want serious.

Neither did he.

Neither *had* he. 'What's your sign?'

'Libra.' She smiled at him and his heart blew wide open.

'Okay.' He peered at the shapes on his phone then found them in the sky and pointed. 'There. You see the upside-down triangle shape?'

She looked up, scrutinising the sky with a frown. 'That looks nothing like weighing scales.'

'Clearly our ancestors weren't that great at drawing shapes.' He shrugged as she laughed. 'Libra. That's September-October, right? Birthday coming up fairly soon. Noted.'

'Don't worry, we'll be well and truly ancient history by then.'

'Ah. Yes. Of course.' It was as if a knife had speared his heart. The end was hurtling towards them and he had a sick feeling in the pit of his stomach at the thought of not having this.

Make the most of it.

That was what he needed to do. Have her. Then let her go. As agreed.

That was what she wanted, right? Hell, he'd

had to talk her into this in the first place. She was probably counting down the days until it was all over.

And yet…he really liked the way she looked at him with such a soft gaze, laughing at his lame jokes, the press of her body against his telling him she wanted him. That wasn't all pretence, was it?

He squeezed her closer. 'If you had a completely free day, what would you do?'

'I'd…' She inhaled deeply then let out the breath slowly as she thought. 'Oh…so much. Depending on the weather. If it was raining, I'd sit in your window seat and read your library's worth of books. Sunshine? I'd spend the day in the mountains, hiking. Riding again. Or I'd do nothing and also do everything I could.'

He laughed into her hair. 'All in one day?'

'Yes. All of it. What would you do?'

Stare at your face. Watch the emotions scud by. Joy. Excitement. Happiness. Satisfaction. Each one with its own special flavour.

A particular shine in her eyes, a certain tug on her lips. The way she almost shook with delight. Hell, happiness looked good on her.

Orgasms did too.

Kissing looked even better, all misty eyes and swollen lips and the secret, sexy smile. His chest filled with that now familiar Ivy warmth and a peculiar kind of pride that he'd made that smile happen just with his mouth. She was intoxicating. Breathtaking.

Whoa.

His mind whirred with a warning alarm.

Given a clear timetable he'd choose to do nothing but *watch her face*? He was starting to think like those romcoms she'd been talking about, and was clearly getting in deeper than he'd expected. And far, far quicker.

He needed to protect himself. Protect them both. Because this stupid deal had brought him closer to Ivy than he'd thought possible. They needed to stop with this soul searching and all this time together. Maybe communicate by text. Or something. Write a list of facts about himself and email it to her to memorise and get her to do the same. Then he wouldn't have to see her beautiful face. Taste her. Touch her. Talk to her. Hold her.

Yes.

No.

That wouldn't work. He'd still see her at work. He had a bad feeling he'd still want her too.

Scratch that. He *would* still want her. He knew that now.

'Lucas?'

'Huh?' He would still want her. Even after all this was over. His belly tightened. His heart started to race.

She poked him again. 'I said, it's your turn. Where is your head at?'

'Here.' He nuzzled her hair, trying to restore some sort of equilibrium in his mind and body. He could create space without hurting her. He was the king of letting women down kindly and with as little fuss as possible. 'I'm right here.'

'So, what would you do if you had a completely free day?'

'I don't know...kite surf. Catch up with mates.'

Her smile fell a little and she sat back. 'Yeah. Actually, I'd catch up with my friends too. Yes.'

He knew she was deflated by his answer, but he couldn't allow her to keep creeping under his skin like this.

A little frown hovered over her forehead as she looked at him. 'Are you okay?'

'Sure.'

She blinked and smiled. 'I just asked if you want to show me how to kite surf.'

'Oh. Sorry.' He'd completely missed that, worrying about how to let her go. 'I don't know.'

'Why not?'

'Because...' He couldn't say what he should say: that teaching her to kite surf was an epically bad idea, because he shouldn't spend any more time with her before the ball. But the words wouldn't come. Instead he said, his tone like that of a little kid greedy for more sugar, 'You'd really want to give it a go?'

She closed one eye and pursed those cute as hell lips as she pondered. 'You took me horse riding so we should do something you like to do. I think we'd get to know each other better in our natural environments.'

'I guess.' So, despite his better judgement, he found himself nodding. It was an outside activity. They couldn't get naked. They couldn't do this…all this intimacy and tenderness, all this kissing and lovemaking, not in crashing waves and cold. Where was the harm in one last outing? At least they'd be able to talk about another shared experience with his parents.

Her eyes narrowed. 'That is, if you think I'll be okay.'

'You'll be fine. Trust me.'

'Hmm…why do I feel nervous when you say that?' She laughed warily, completely oblivious to the turmoil swirling in his head.

He shrugged. 'I'm a pro. I've got your back.'

But he figured she was right. Trusting him was a very unwise thing to do.

It was becoming a habit now, walking onto the ward and hoping he was here, her tummy all excited with anticipation. Then riding the wave of disappointment when he wasn't. Four days since their wonderful day and she hadn't run into him, even though they shared the same patient. Seemed like either he was avoiding her or their schedules just hadn't coincided. She supposed she could call him or text him, but that wasn't their way. Yet.

But her belly danced as she spied the top of his head sticking out over the nurses' station desk in the centre of the ward. Suddenly her day got a whole lot brighter. 'Hey, Lucas.'

He looked up and grinned. 'Ivy. Looking great.'

She felt the blush creep up her cheeks. Not that anyone was listening, but she wasn't used to compliments at work. Or this endless ache to kiss him again. Just be with him. She shook herself. 'How's things?'

He pointed to the computer monitor. 'Just writing Emma's notes up.'

'Oh, how's she doing post-surgery?'

'It's early days, but she's in good spirits. The partial thickness grafts are healing well and the donor sites are looking great too. The full thickness grafts aren't causing her much more pain but make movement limited.'

'That will improve though?'

'Absolutely, with time and physiotherapy. I'd be really happy to get her to a stage where she can hold those twins on her lap when they're born. We haven't looked under the pressure dressings yet. I'm hopeful they're doing their job and I'm just glad we didn't have to wait any longer.'

Then he would discharge Emma and there'd be no more need for them to bump into each other here. Ivy's heart jittered. 'Quick question.'

His eyebrows peaked. 'Sure?'

'What's the actual dress code for the ball?'

'Man, you looked so serious for a minute I was starting to panic.' He laughed. 'Sorry, I haven't shown you the invitation. It's black tie. Ball gowns.'

'Okay. So the last time I went to a ball was probably after my graduation. Looks like I'm going to have to go shopping.'

'If you need any help, let me know.'

'Lucas, you are not coming shopping with me. I have girlfriends to do that with. It'll make a fun afternoon. I haven't seen them all for ages.'

'Okay.' He tugged her hand and pulled her down level with his face, lowering his voice to a tantalising teasing whisper. 'Too bad, I wanted to be in that fitting room with you. Now I'll just have to imagine you naked.'

'Lucas!' She lowered her voice too. 'I will have underwear on. No one tries on clothes without it. Ugh.'

'That is a big shame.' He mock-pouted.

'Not for me.' She straightened, all the better to keep the professional guise on. 'You still okay for kite surfing?'

'Certainly am. The weather forecast looks perfect but you'll need a wetsuit.'

She grinned and did a ticking motion with her hand. 'Check.'

'Excellent.' He tugged her down again, making her laugh. 'I will imagine you naked under that instead.'

'Ugh. All that rubber on my tender bits? Talk about chafing. No, thank you.'

'Aww, not into rubber?' He eyed her suspiciously, making her chuckle.

She put her palm on his cheek. 'Is it all just about sex with you?'

'Sure is.' His grin was good enough to kiss.

But she withdrew her hand in case she was drawn into temptation. Not here. Not at work. 'Good.'

'I'll pick you up at eight again.'

An idea occurred to her. 'You could…no. Sorry. Forget it.'

He frowned. 'What?'

'Nothing.'

'Come on, spit it out.' He glanced around. It was the patients' lunchtime and the staff were busy. 'No one can hear you. Is it about rubber? Getting naked?'

She couldn't help laughing and bugging her eyes at him. 'No. Well…maybe… I was just thinking you could come over for pizza on Friday night. Then we could head out to the beach together Saturday morning.' This was not what they did. The physical intimacy had been spontaneous so far. If he brought spare clothes and a toothbrush, if they planned cosy nights in, what would that mean?

He hesitated, as if thinking the same thing.

Ugh. She'd said the wrong thing. Thought the wrong thing. It was just about the sex and not about staying the night. Even after the horse riding and going back to his amazing apartment she'd eventually headed home to sleep. 'Like I said, forget it.'

He looked blindsided. Shook his head. 'No. It's just—'

'Ivy?' It was Alinta. Strolling towards her and grinning an *'Ivy and Lucas sitting in a tree'* kind of teasing smile.

Bad timing, girlfriend.

But she was still pleased to see her. If for nothing more than moral support to bolster her against Lucas's brief hesitant grimace. Had it been a grimace?

'Hey, Ali, it's been ages. How's things?' Ivy glanced at Lucas and she still couldn't read his expression. Was he working out how to let her down gently? 'Do you know Lucas Matthews?'

'From a distance.' Ali nodded in greeting. 'Hi. Alinta Edwards. Head of Obstetrics and Gynaecology.'

Was it her imagination or did Lucas looked relieved to have someone else here? It was probably her imagination, right? But maybe he really didn't want to spend the night. It seemed as if second-guessing had become her superpower.

He nodded back and smiled. 'Good to meet you, Ali.'

'I'm here to see Emma for her antenatal check,' Ali said. 'Any chance of a quick update?'

'All looking good from my end. The actual appendectomy shouldn't have caused any labour risk, but the new incision scars are still healing. Lucas has just been filling me in on her grafts too,' Ivy encouraged him to add any more information.

'They're healing well. If she continues improving like this, she'll be discharged from in-patient care with us. We'll just keep going with the dressings in the community with outpatient follow-up. And physiotherapy, of course.' He smiled his winning smile. 'She's come a long way.'

Ali blew out a slow breath. 'And has been through so many hospital specialties. Poor woman.'

'Here's hoping things keep heading in the right direction after her few hiccups.' Lucas looked at his watch. 'Sorry, but I've got a surgery starting soon. I need to dash. If you need any more info from me let me know. I'm happy to chat any time.'

'Nice to meet you properly.' Ali smiled, then as Lucas walked away she side-mouthed, 'Hubba-

hubba. What's this I've been hearing about you and the delectable Dr Matthews?'

'What?' Ivy's heart drummed against her ribcage.

'Phoebe may have mentioned a certain deal you have going with that particular reconstructive surgeon.' Oh, her bestie was grinning now. 'Was it okay for her to tell me?'

'Of course. I can't have secrets from you guys, right? I would have told you myself, but I've been busy.'

'With the aforementioned reconstructive surgeon.' Ali bugged her eyes and laughed.

'Maybe. But also work.' To prove her point, Ivy shuffled the papers on the desk. Although it was really more for something to do with her hands, and to stop her looking at Ali and getting the expected knowing looks. And then having to admit she was in just a little bit deeper with Lucas than she'd planned to be.

Ali waved her hand dismissively. 'Work schmirk. You can admit he's hot, you know. Because he is. Seems nice too.'

Ivy decided not to encourage that conversation any further. 'Actually, I have an…issue I need to discuss with you.'

'Oh, my God, what? You need an obstetrician. You're pregnant? With him?' Ali looked shocked. Even though she was an obstetrician she'd never expressed a desire to have children of her own.

None of her friends here had them. They'd all been too consumed with work and life and…the lack of suitable men and never the right timing. 'Honestly. No. I need a ball gown for a gala ball.'

'Phew.' Ali sighed and grinned. 'You had me concerned for a minute. Okay. Yes. Leave it with me. I'll rally the troops. We'll come and help you choose one. Saturday?'

'I can't. I'm going kite surfing.' Ivy picked up the papers now and refused to look Alinta in the eye at this admission. Her friends knew she was more of a land lubber than a fish.

'Say what?' Ali's eyes almost popped out of her head.

'Kite surfing. You know. Ocean. Sail. Board.'

'Why?'

'Apparently it's fun.'

'It's also cold and wet and winter. Oh… I get it. It's a date. A wet date. Then you can warm up together.' Ali pulled a cheesy face, unwittingly getting to the heart of it all. 'Cute.'

Ivy bristled. She was so busted. 'Not a date. We're just getting to know each other so we can fool his family into believing we're together.'

'You can do that in a cafe. Or over the phone. By email. I know you, Ivy Hurst. There is no way you'd do anything as extreme as kite surfing if it wasn't a date.'

Alinta had a point. But Ivy had just wanted

to do something Lucas was interested in so she could see him in his comfort zone. 'It's research.'

'Okay. Dress it up however you want. Lie to me. Just don't lie to yourself.'

'How is everyone into my business so much? I'm a grown woman completely in control. And I'm not lying.'

'Hmm.' Ali shot her a disbelieving look. 'Well, I can't do Sunday so…'

'How about next week Saturday? That'll still give me a week before the ball.'

'Okay. It's a date. Have fun in the ocean and…' Ali's eyes narrowed and she gave her a pointed look. 'Be. Careful.'

'I can swim just fine.'

'I wasn't talking about swimming.'

Ivy sighed. *Here we go again.* 'Oh, honestly. Why does everyone keep telling me to be careful?'

Ali wrapped an arm over Ivy's shoulder and hugged her close. 'Because we love you and don't want you to get hurt. We saw what Grant did to you and don't ever want to see you that upset again.'

'You sound just like Phoebe. It's kite surfing, Ali. There is nothing intimate about that. The only thing that might get hurt is my pride when I'm rubbish at it and get dumped in the water. Definitely not my heart. I'm immune to him, okay?' Even as she said the words she knew they weren't true. She was far from immune. She liked him, for goodness' sake. She liked him a lot.

Too much.

'Immune to a hunk of a man, all wet and pumping muscles? A rub-down with a towel? Or…a spa to warm you both up? Not to mention the way you watched him leave as if you wanted to go with him. Or eat him…whichever you got a chance to do first.' Alinta stepped away and frowned as she spoke. 'Come on, Ivy.'

'What?' Ivy put her palms up in submission and dug deep for a laugh. Because she knew Ali was right and that her friends cared deeply for her. And she loved them for it. 'We're not dating, okay?'

No matter how much she wanted to. Because, yes…okay, she wanted to date him. She didn't want this to end and she was fairly sure he couldn't wait until the ball and be done with her. She'd seen that hesitation. He didn't want to stay the night. He was more than happy for a booty call and she had been too. But…but something had changed. For her at least.

But there was no point wanting what she couldn't have. She'd done that too many times with Grant in the past. With her family too. She wasn't going to willingly walk into a situation where she could be rejected all over again.

Alinta's eyebrows gathered in. 'Hey, I'm sorry. I was just joking around. Are you okay?'

Ivy inhaled deeply then blew out slowly. There was no point in getting upset about things going exactly to plan. Although she was having a hard time convincing her pining heart of that. 'I'm fine. I'm absolutely fine.'

If she said it enough, she might just believe it.

CHAPTER TEN

LUCAS KNOCKED AT the door of Ivy's apartment, his heart giddy, waiting for her to answer.

She opened it a smidgeon as if assessing who might be calling round on a Friday evening. When she saw him, her eyes widened but there wasn't much of a smile as she said, 'Oh, hi, Lucas. I was just about to text you. I wasn't sure what we'd agreed.'

To be honest, he hadn't been sure either. When she'd asked him to stay over, he'd hesitated because he'd immediately wanted to scream *hell, yes*. A whole night with her? Holding her? Kissing her? Waking up with her? Morning sex?

But the sensible part of his brain had suggested he calm right down. It had been the same when she'd said, *'I am not in the habit of kissing one guy when I want to be with someone else.'*

God help him, but he'd slid into that proclamation with so many emotions and all of them at odds with each other. Excitement. Panic. Want. Fear. Desire.

And even now he was grappling with the aftershocks. Ivy was compelling and alluring and… it almost felt too easy. Too comfortable. And yet wildly exhilarating at the same time. And that made him want to do things he'd always refused to do, like stay the night.

In the end, he'd decided to just ignore his brain and do what she'd suggested, but he wasn't sure she was overly excited at seeing him. Had he messed up by not being more definite? Should he have phoned first? Committed?

Ugh. Such a loaded word. Committed to having fun, yes. He held up his overnight bag and the pizza box. 'Dinner and a sleepover, right? Like teenage girls.'

She grimaced but the corners of her mouth did turn up a little. 'I sincerely hope not.'

'Aw, no pillow fights and painting our toenails?'

A hesitant smile. 'If you really want to.'

Yes, he should have phoned. 'Can I come in?'

She peered at the holdall hooked in his fingers. 'What's in the bag?'

'Toothbrush. Toiletries. PJs. Couple of bottles of wine. Red and white because I wasn't sure which you'd prefer.'

Her eyes widened. 'You wear pyjamas?'

'Not if I can help it. But you know…just in case it was cold.'

'Oh, don't worry, Lucas. It won't be cold.' Finally grinning, she opened the door wider. She was dressed casually in a T-shirt and shorts, her shapely legs attracting his attention as he followed her into her kitchen and put the pizza on the table, his bag on the floor. Then he turned to her.

She stared up at him. Gone was her hesitation. Yeah…there was an irony in the fact she was now the hesitant one. But she was looking at him with something akin to affection. Desire. As if he were a gift on her birthday.

He stroked her cheek. 'I should have phoned. I'm sorry.'

She nodded. 'I might have made other plans, so yes, a quick call would have been better. Wouldn't want that pizza to have gone to waste.'

'Other plans?' He didn't like the sound of that.

A shrug. 'Yes, Lucas. You are not the only person I want to spend time with.'

'Aw, heck, Ivy.' He tugged her closer and kissed that tender spot behind her ear. Then slicked a trail of kisses across her lips, making her moan against his mouth. 'But I'm the only person who does this to you.'

'Maybe…' She laughed and tapped the side of her nose. 'Maybe not.'

He tried to ignore the cleave in his chest at the thought of her with anyone else. Of another man touching her, kissing her. He was pretty damn sure there wasn't anyone else—hadn't she all but said she was a one-man woman? She was just teasing. ‘Come on. Tell me who else makes you feel this hot.’

He claimed her mouth again, long and slow until she was writhing against him. ‘Okay, okay. I’m glad you’re here, Lucas.’

‘Me too.’

There was some slow and sweet R & B music playing softly through her kitchen speakers. Her hair was rumpled as if she’d been sleeping or lying down, maybe reading a book? The book he’d given her? There was something wholesome and just damned good about that image. Her eyes were clear and bright. Her smile was sexy as hell. Wordlessly, she reached for his hand and interlaced her fingers between his. It was such a simple gesture, but deeply intimate. He didn’t hold hands.

But his heart caught. His skin tightened. He relaxed and yet grew excited all at the same time. She stroked her fingers against his then lifted his hand to her lips and kissed them. Such a simple action but it felt pure, reverential. He brought their hands to his mouth and kissed them too, then kissed her palm, the inside of her wrist, the dip in her elbow. Everything felt slowed down, each second elongated. Pure. It was one of those moments he knew he’d tuck tight into his memory banks and keep revisiting.

Her eyes flickered closed as he reached her

collarbone and pressed a trail of kisses there too. He noted the dancing pulse in her throat as he kissed her jawline. Then, because he simply couldn't wait any longer, he slid his mouth over hers again.

His heart swelled as he tasted her, as she responded with the tight, firm press of her body, the trail of her fingertips down his cheek. He'd been struggling with coming here tonight with the promise of increased intimacy, but he'd omitted that she would feel so good, taste so good.

'Lucas.' It was a throaty gasp that touched every part of him.

Sound so good.

How could he have thought about denying himself this? 'Bedroom.'

'Yes.' Her voice was shaky and desperate, and she grasped at his jacket lapels. 'I need you inside me. It's been too long.'

'Five days, twenty-two hours and too many minutes.' It shocked him that he knew that, that he'd been subconsciously counting down the time until he could do this again. He'd hesitated when she'd asked him to stay. His brain had silenced him. What a damned fool.

'Too long.' She grabbed his hand and rushed him to her bedroom. Threw off her clothes and dragged his off too. Within moments he was sheathed and nudging into her.

The only place he wanted to be.

* * *

After, he kissed her long and slow, sated and satisfied but eager for more. She looked dazed and sleepy as he nestled her into the crook of his arm. He rested his cheek on the top of her head. 'That's better. So very much better.'

She chuckled against his chest. 'Bad day?'

'No, actually. A good day.' And getting better by the second. 'You?'

'Awful.' She pulled a face, wrinkling her nose. 'I had to tell a twenty-two-year-old they had bowel cancer today. It sucks.'

'Wow. That's so young.'

'It happens, sadly. He's an apprentice electrician. Just an ordinary guy. Kid really. He reminded me of Sione. All barely there facial hair, too long limbs that he was still growing into, an innocence I was crushing with the worst kind of news. And then he was all over the place. At first, he tried to make jokes about it. Then, as it sank in, he was incredulous. Then, when he heard about the treatment and his survival chances, he got angry. Trying so hard not to cry. So, so hard not to be seen as anything other than strong and brave.' Her mouth turned down. 'Which made me kind of wobble—'

'Hey, I know. I know exactly what you're saying. I've been there too many times. You have such compassion and a tender heart.' He stroked her cheek, tilted her chin and kissed her nose, her eyelids, her mouth.

Tears swam in her eyes and his own heart twisted. 'You want to tell me all about it?'

'It's fine. Grant always said we should leave work at work.' She swallowed and, with a wonky smile, shook her head. He knew it was an act of bravado.

'I'm not Grant.' He tried not to growl but the mention of that idiot who had treated her with such disrespect threatened to bring down his mood. 'Talk.'

So, she did. She lay in his arms and told him about her patient's hopes of being in a rock band and that his parents had told him he needed a proper job, so he'd started his electrician training. And how he was regretting that now and wished he'd followed his dreams instead of toeing his parents' line.

'I hear that a lot,' Lucas agreed. 'People doing things…spending lifetimes doing things…because it's expected, or they think it's the right thing to do. But for who? It's one thing to take other people's wants and needs into consideration, but you have to live your life for yourself. Makes me so glad that I struck out against the family dictate.'

'Me too.' Her fingertips ran across his chest. 'And yet, I also hear people wishing they'd mended the family feuds and been closer to their people. I wish things didn't have to be so complicated.'

'What exactly happened with you and your parents?'

Her shoulders slumped a little. 'They said I could be an army medic if I was so invested in being a doctor. That our life was about duty and service. That army life was all I'd known and I'd struggle with anything different. That they understood sacrifice but also that it was an honour to serve. But I was going through a rocky, possibly rebellious, phase.' She shot him a rueful smile. 'Definitely rebellious. You know me, light and dark. And I told them where to stick their service. That I wanted to be free from rules and orders.'

'Which explains a little of why you barked at me when you thought I'd given you an order that night in your office.' He chuckled at the memory. She'd been so fierce and vivid and vibrant that his interest—and libido—had been off the scale. Seemed that now he knew her better, she was all those things and so much more too, that his interest and libido hadn't waned at all. In fact, they'd both hit new heights.

She laughed. 'Yeah. I don't like being told what to do and not be allowed to discuss options. Living that army life didn't feel like an honour to me, it felt as though they had no control over their lives. I guess, looking back, I was blinded by my own subjectivity, because it's not really like that. They have a lot of autonomy while doing a very important job that needs boundaries and rules. But I didn't see it like that back then, I just wanted to be free. We had a huge argument, and they threw me out, saying I was ungrateful and spiteful and thought I was better than them.'

'That's hard.'

'It is.' Her eyes misted. 'Things have never been right ever since. Oh, we talk a couple of times a year to catch up on everyone's news but there's a distance between us that I'm not sure we'll ever overcome. We have different values and beliefs and desires. Different perspectives. I love them, but I don't necessarily like them for barking orders at me and expecting me to follow through.'

'I don't blame you. Well done for having the courage to walk away. That was brave.'

'Not brave. Desperate. I couldn't stay. I refused to do what they told me to do. I had no choice.'

'You became a doctor and you save lives, you make people better, you make their lives better. Your friends' lives too. And mine.' He swallowed. Hell, what was he saying? He couldn't encourage any further intimacy on this kind of level, but the sentiments kept tripping out of his mouth.

'Lucas?' She stared up at him and smiled, fingers grazing his jaw. 'Thank you.'

'For what?'

'Being you.'

Whoa. No one had ever said anything so heartfelt like that to him either. And it seemed to come as easy to her as it did to him. They had a tight connection on so many levels. Respect, fun, attraction, shared interests.

A man could fall into this, he thought. Maybe too deep and too hard and lose himself in the dream. And then she'd realise he wasn't all she thought he was. That he couldn't keep her safe. That he couldn't be trusted.

A dark shadow scudded across his chest. He needed to distract himself, so he sat up and dragged a pillow from behind. Took aim and whacked her gently on her arm.

'What the actual…? Lucas!' But she was still laughing and reaching for her pillow now.

'Sleepover pillow fight. Bring it on.'

'Oh, I'm going to bring it.' She knelt up and thwacked him with her pillow across the side of his face.

He took it and laughed. 'Right. This is war.' Then hit her legs, making her squeal.

'Lucas Matthews. You are so dead.' She hit him in the belly, but must have lost her balance because all of a sudden she was tilting towards him, screaming with laughter.

He tickled her just under her ribs until she was rolling on the bed, tears streaming down her face. 'I surrender! Surrender!'

'Aha.' He guffawed and pulled her closer so she couldn't wriggle away. 'Captured.'

'Help,' she whispered, grinning and looking the least scared anyone had looked ever. More, the expression on her face...of fun, affection and promises...hell, she was getting involved here. He couldn't let that happen. He couldn't have her hoping for more once this deal was done.

But it was he who hadn't been able to resist the pull of a sleepover. He who had ached to slide inside her. Be with her. He who yearned for this comfortable ease between them, and the wild sex too. So, in truth, it was he who was captured and captivated.

It was getting too much for his heart and his hopes. Man, hopes he'd never allowed himself to have before. Hopes he most certainly didn't deserve. He needed to slow it all down. But he didn't know how.

He slicked a kiss on the tip of her nose as her belly growled loudly. 'Hungry?'

She covered her stomach with her hand and giggled. 'Starving. I don't think I've eaten anything since breakfast.'

'Then stay here and I'll bring up a picnic.'

And in the meantime, try to wrestle these emotions into some kind of order.

* * *

He'd actually turned up. She hadn't known how to feel when she'd opened the door. Relief that he was here? Frustration that he hadn't confirmed beforehand?

Excitement. Yes, definitely that.

Then he'd showed her how much he'd missed her. And her heart was full again. Because the feeling had been entirely mutual. A craving to have him close, to be connected again instead of snatched conversations at work, watching him walk away from her. This time together was special.

Lucas returned with a tray of reheated pizza, two wine glasses and a bottle of chardonnay, which he placed onto the middle of her bed then bowed low, a tea towel over his arm. A bath towel, slung low around his slim waist, showcased his flat abs and that delicious arrow of hair that pointed lower and promised so much. He most certainly looked more appetising than the food.

He made a *ta-dah* motion with his hands. 'Dinner is served, ma'am. I wasn't sure what pizza you'd like so I took a punt on margherita.'

'Anything, as long as it's not got pine—'

'Pineapple?' he said at the same time she did.

'Great minds.' She reached for a piece of pizza, constantly amazed at just how in sync they were. 'Pineapple on pizza is the devil's food.'

'Never, ever put fruit on pizza.' He snatched a piece and chinked it with hers. 'Deal?'

'Deal.'

He grinned and nodded, playful and just so gorgeous her limbs felt weak just from her looking at him. 'And never anchovies.'

She shuddered at the thought. 'Absolutely not. I promise never anchovies.'

It felt as if they were planning ahead here. Beyond what they'd agreed.

Her phone rang. She leaned over and grabbed her shorts from the floor where she'd left them in her eagerness to have Lucas in her bed. Dug her phone out of the pocket and looked at the screen, unsure whether to take the call. 'It's Harper.'

He nodded. 'Take it.'

'Are you sure?'

'You said you don't catch up often enough. Take it. I can wait.' He caught her dubious expression and nodded. 'Honestly. Please, talk to her. I'll just fill my belly here.'

'Save me another piece. I promise I won't be long.' She slid to the edge of the bed and turned away to talk to her friend, aware of his gaze on her and wanting to hurry up to get back to their evening together. Which made her feel like a bad friend. But she didn't have much longer for this whatever it was with Lucas. Her mood took a little nosedive so she forced jollity into her tone. 'Hey, Harper. How's you?'

'Good. Great. Fantastic! I have news.' Her friend sounded breathless.

'What kind of news?' It was so good to hear her sound so cheerful after everything she'd been through caring for Yarran and his burns, finding her way back to him.

'I…well, I asked Yarran to marry me.'

'Oh, my God! No! You didn't? He said yes?'

'He said yes.' Harper's voice was filled with happiness.

'Wow! I'm so happy for you. I can't believe it, after all this time.' Ivy held the phone between her chin and shoulder and turned to Lucas, pointing to her left-hand ring finger.

His dark eyes flared with surprise, but he didn't look as excited as she was. But then, he didn't know Harper and Yarran or their history, hadn't lived through the break-up, supported them both.

Or was he just against relationships? And why?

Why?

And why did it matter so much?

She turned back to talk to Harper. 'Have you got a date planned?'

'No. We're going shopping for the rings tomorrow. But we're not rushing into getting married just yet. We need to wait until Yarran's fully healed and, well, just wallow in being an engaged couple.'

'I am so happy for you.' Yet her heart felt heavy and she couldn't quite put her finger on why.

But she had a niggling idea that it had something to do with Lucas's expression. She finished the conversation then turned back to him. 'So Harper asked Yarran to marry her.'

He was leaning back against the headboard, arms crossed. 'I guessed as much. She asked him?'

'Yes. I imagine it was the best way to show him she loves him and how committed she is.'

'But that's a bit quick, right? They haven't been together very long.'

'Well, yes and no. Yes, because they've only recently got together. No, because they were almost engaged twelve years ago, before Harper upped and left to go to London. They're going to go shopping for rings, but apparently waiting for a while before they actually get married.' She noticed a frown forming deep over his eyes. 'What is it?'

He shook his head. 'What's what?'

'Why are you frowning?'

'I'm not.' His features rearranged into a smile that lit his mouth but not his eyes. 'You seem very excited over the prospect of a wedding.'

'Their wedding, yes. She's one of my best friends and I'm thrilled she's so happy, at last. I'm sure you were happy about George and Ivan?'

'Knowing about George's inability to commit, it was a surprise but…' His eyebrows rose and he gave an empty laugh. 'A happy one, I guess.'

I guess?

A pause she didn't know how to fill yawned between them. Something didn't feel quite right here. The vibe had changed. He was too quiet. Was he against marriage full stop or just against *him* getting married?

Then he sat forward. 'Why didn't you and Grant get married? Oh, *were* you married?'

She laughed at the thought. 'It just never happened, thank goodness. That would have made everything even more messy. We talked about it, of course. But we were so busy with our jobs and building our careers we never got to the engagement stage.' In hindsight she realised she probably didn't want it enough for her to make it happen. 'I've learnt from that, though. If you want to be with someone you need to make them know it. You have to make that commitment and act on it.'

He nodded but the light in his eyes had definitely dimmed. 'I guess so.'

'You never wanted to get married?'

He gave a sharp shake of his head. Flat mouth. 'No.'

'That's it? Just no?'

'Just no, Ivy.'

She scrambled backwards up the bed and sat

next to him, her head against the headboard too. But despite their proximity and the warm air coming from the heat pump she felt suddenly alone and cold.

Which didn't make sense. They were in this for another couple of weeks. She'd known that going in. They were doing exactly what they'd agreed. Whether Lucas wanted to get married or not, wanted to commit to someone or not, was none of her business. She was just fine. She had never given marriage to him a thought. She had exactly what she wanted here with a no-strings affair.

So why was her heart hurting?

CHAPTER ELEVEN

'It's freezing.' Ivy was sitting next to him on the beach, tugging a long wetsuit up her gorgeous legs. Goosebumps mushroomed across her beautiful skin. 'Why did I agree to this?'

He laughed, reaching back behind his shoulder to pull up his wetsuit zip. 'I did warn you. You could have stayed at home in that nice warm bed. We could have been doing something very different from this.'

She turned, face red with the effort of wrestling the neoprene, and grinned. Clearly very aware of what he was referring to. 'And miss the chance to see you in your happy place? Surely, you've brought a regular girlfriend here before? Not just this fake one?'

His heart tightened. This wasn't fake. Being here, doing this. Enjoying her company. Last night. Sleeping over. Not fake at all. Very real, in fact.

He shook his head, hoping the panic wasn't obvious in his expression. 'Nope. Not one.'

'Why not?'

He shrugged, choosing not to spell it out to her again: he didn't have girlfriends. Just dates. Just…sex really. 'It just never happened.'

Truth was, he'd almost not brought her here today. Had scrambled around for excuses but come up with nothing convincing. Plus, the temptation to be around her was as compelling as ever, despite the strange feeling in his chest when she'd talked about marriage.

Hell, she hadn't even been talking about their marriage. But it was balled up with the commitment thing, right? Long term. For ever stuff. Depending on someone, trusting them to hold your heart, and your dreams, wishes and hopes safe.

Geez, he couldn't even keep his sister physically safe, never mind anything else. And if he couldn't do it for her—someone he adored—how on earth could he do it for someone else?

Yet, here he was, doing this anyway because he wanted to make Ivy smile and the chances of spending more time with her were getting fewer and fewer as time zipped on, hurtling towards the ball. The end.

She knelt and wriggled the wetsuit over her hips and breasts then slid her arms in, shuffled back towards him. 'Zip me up?'

'Sure.' But it was too easy to slowly tug the zip down and slide his hands across her belly, to rake his fingers across her skin, delighting in the way she shivered against him.

'Lucas,' she whispered, his name whipping into the breeze, her gaze intent on the horizon, her expression serious.

He leaned his chin on her shoulder, heart thumping as he wondered what she was going to say. 'Ivy?'

'Take your freezing hands out of my wetsuit or there'll be no more sex for you. Not even a little bit.'

'You wouldn't dare.'

'Don't push me.' She laughed and twisted round so he had to quickly slide his hands out from her waist or risk two broken wrists.

'Wow, you really meant it.' He laughed too, because there'd really been no danger.

'I just hate being cold.' She bugged her eyes at him.

'Then you've come to the wrong place.' He jumped up before he stripped her naked and made love to her right here on this beach, which, given it was nine o'clock in the morning and already pretty busy, was not a good idea. 'Come on, let's get in the water. We'll start in the shallows first, so you get the hang of it.'

After he pumped up the leading edge and ran through the basics with her he took her knee-deep into the water. Showed her how to check that the lines were all separated, secured her safety harness and launched the kite. He then ran through how to relaunch once more.

Her hands literally shook with what he discovered was impatience. 'Yes. Yes. I understand all that. When do I get to board?'

'Patience, young Padawan. I need you to be safe and know how to get back to the beach. We don't want you ending up in New Zealand with a sharp gust of wind you can't control.'

'How do I get good enough to try the board?'

'You need to make your turns into the wind window a little sharper. More aggressive. Then you can get yourself from body dragging to body surfing.'

She grinned and grabbed hold of the leading edge again. 'Bring it. Let's go.'

Once she'd mastered control of the kite, he let her try with her feet on a board.

She was bent forward, water gushing into her face as the kite rushed her forward a few feet. 'Oh, my God! This is epic.'

'Lean back so you don't swallow half the ocean. Now you feel comfortable on the edge of the wind window, scoop your wings a little deeper. You'll fly in no time.'

He towed her out deeper. Kissed her cheek and let her go. 'Careful. Careful. Hold on.'

There was too much for her to remember all in one go. The wings dipped and scooped, but not enough. She didn't lean enough into the wind.

Then she did. 'Ivy! Go! You got it! You did it!'

'Yay!' Her happy screeches floated across the bay. She let go with one hand and pumped her fist triumphantly in the air. His heart jolted with pride as if it fist-bumped right back. He watched her skim across the tops of the waves and his chest contracted with respect and admiration. Maybe more. He liked this woman. Really liked her. And he knew she liked him.

For a moment he metaphorically rode that excitement with her. Letting his imagination run wild with long nights and early mornings. With togetherness and sharing things, memories, life. Love.

His heart tangled itself around the vision of her fist-pumping the blue sky, harnessing an invisible power that was bigger than both of them. How hard would it be to let himself fall into something like that? With someone like her? How hard would it be to start trusting himself?

She met him back on the sand as they'd agreed, letting the breeze push her into the wash. He ran to her and she jumped up and down. 'I did it! I did it!'

'Way to go! I am so proud of you.' He picked her up and whirled her round in a circle.

She put her hands on his shoulders and kissed him quickly. But he wasn't going to let her go that soon. 'Come here,' he growled and pulled her flat against him, capturing her mouth. She tasted of salt and fresh air, elemental and happy. Yes, she tasted happy.

He pulled away, desperate to know if she felt the way she tasted. 'And?'

'It was amazing. I was flying. I was actually flying.' She put her hand to her heart. 'I think I've just had a religious experience.'

Well, she'd only barely lifted off the water, but he wasn't going to burst her bubble. 'You were awesome. You're a natural.'

'I love it.' Eyes shining brightly, she kissed him again. 'Thank you, Lucas. It is the best thing ever.'

Thank you.

She kept saying that. As if the things he did for her really mattered. He tucked it away into the Ivy corner of his heart.

'The pleasure was one hundred per cent mine.' He glanced at his watch, thinking that some cold water might help douse these tussling emotions. 'One more go before we head back? Tide's going to turn soon, and it'll make things more difficult for you.'

'Only if you come in too and I can watch you do some tricks.'

Oh, no. He was staying where he could see her. 'I won't be able to watch out for you properly if I'm not here. It's best if I stay on the beach, then, when you come in, I'll go out.'

She frowned and jabbed him in the ribs. 'Oh,

come on. It'll be fine. The wind's practically shoving us towards the beach anyway.'

'No, Ivy.'

'Come on. You told me you love doing it. I want to see you excited by something.'

He stroked his fingers down her breasts. 'Here. These.'

She captured his fingers in hers. 'Something *else*. I can't talk to your mum about your breast obsession, can I? Come on. Just for five minutes. I want to see you fly too.'

'No.'

'Scared? Have you been lying to me all along? You can't really do this stuff, can you?' She was teasing, but it hit a nerve.

'Sure, I can.'

'Then prove it.'

She wanted to watch him. Wanted him to teach her. And hell, that was such a powerful punch to his chest he couldn't resist basking in the glory of her gaze. 'Okay. Just one trick. As long as you stay in the shallows where you'll be safe.'

She jumped up and down and clapped her hands. 'Yay! Now I get to see the professional in action.'

So, he launched her kite, then his. Made sure she was up and steady then blew her a kiss as he harnessed the full power of the wind, shouting, 'Don't try this at home!'

He flew across the tops of the waves, heading

sharp east, jumped and turned, making a quick grab of his board because it always looked harder and more impressive than it was, and then aimed to head back to her, sharp west. As he turned he tried to spot her in the shallows. But she wasn't there.

Damn.

Where was she?

He scanned the water. She wasn't there. He steered towards the spot where he'd left her and caught sight of her crawling on her hands and knees along the shallows dragging the kite behind her.

She was hurt.

His stomach lurched up into his throat.

No.

No.

Too-familiar feelings of panic roiled in his gut and swelled through his chest.

He steered onto the beach and ran across the sand, his heart firing like rapid rifle shot against his ribcage. 'Ivy. Ivy, are you okay?'

'I'm…' She put her palm on her forehead and winced. 'I hope I don't have a bruise for the ball.'

'Hot damn, Ivy. I don't care about the ball.'

I care about you.

Yeah, he'd probably known that for a long time. But this was the first time he was admitting it.

He knelt in front of her and checked her over. Why had he been showing off?

Why had he let her talk him into going on the water when she was there? Why had he been so distracted to the point of not looking out for her?

Why…why…why? The same question that had run through his head so many times over the years like a song playing on repeat, the ear worm was always there. He'd thought he'd learnt about making stupid decisions, but obviously not.

Bile rose in his throat and he turned away from the bump he might as well have caused.

And there it was. Exactly why he shouldn't be allowed around people he cared about. Because when he stuffed up, he did it big time. He shouldn't have been fooling around to impress her, he should have been focused on making sure she was okay. Hadn't he already learnt that lesson?

He pushed her wet hair away from her forehead and gently examined the lump on her head. 'What happened?'

'I don't know. I think I caught too much wind. I panicked. The lines got tangled and I lifted off, somehow lost the board, which went flying and hit me on the head on its way back down.'

He started to untangle the lines and removed the safety harness from her waist in an effort to stop his hands shaking limply by his sides. 'Damn, Ivy.'

She flinched as if she'd been hit a second time. 'What?'

He changed the tone, lowering his voice, not wanting to make her feel any worse. 'Just damn and hell.'

'Lucas?'

Stupid. Careless. This is all your fault.

'Lucas. Look at me.'

His jaw stiffened and he ground his teeth together.

'Lucas. I'm fine. What's wrong?'

He shook his head until he had enough control over his emotions that he could look at her again. 'I shouldn't have been showing off like that. I should have been on the beach watching your every move. Out there I can't keep you safe.'

'It was just a gust of wind. An accident. You are not responsible for me, Lucas.'

'I am. You're…'

'Go on.' Her eyes bugged at him. 'What am I exactly?'

Everything.

These thoughts kept pelting him from all angles. He cared for her. She meant so much to him. Too much. Which was stupid and dangerous, but he couldn't keep away. Ached for her approval, her respect and admiration. And now look what had happened. She'd got hurt. 'This is my gig, Ivy. I'm supposed to look after you.'

'No, you're not. I can look after myself quite

well, thanks. You were just teaching me how to kite surf. And it's only a small bump.' But she looked at him as if she were trying to solve a math equation or something. Trying to work him out.

Good luck with that.

'You're not going back in again.'

She frowned, putting the skin on her forehead under more pressure. Then winced. 'I beg your pardon?'

'We're going home.'

'Lucas, no. Stop.' She held up her palm, body taut and expression as fierce as that first evening together when she'd pushed her office chair at him. 'I don't know what you're thinking or who you think you are, but you're not the boss of me, and you certainly don't get to tell me what I can or can't do. If I want to go back in the water, I will. If I don't want to, then I won't. You're over-reacting here.'

'I'm not.' Great, and now they were having an argument and that was his fault too. 'You know we can stop this any time, Ivy. You've already got your prize.' The words tumbled out of him. Self-preservation probably. But it was rude and unthinking. A gut reaction.

'What? I have one stupid, minor accident while learning to do a thing I've never done be-fore and you want to call the whole thing off? You don't want to keep going until the ball because I hit my head?' Her eyes shimmered with hurt and he hated himself for causing that. 'I don't understand.'

'I'm just saying I won't hold you to it.'

'Wow, Lucas. Are you trying to get rid of me all of a sudden?'

'Just giving you options.'

'Options?' Her mouth dropped open as her eyebrows peaked. 'To stick to my word or cry off. Is that what you want? You want me to leave? Where is this coming from?'

'I just want to let you off the hook with this stupid deal. Grant thinks you're awesome again. I can manage my mother if needs be.'

'Whoa. I'm not a quitter, Lucas. I made you a promise.' She ran her fingertips over the red lump on her forehead. 'This isn't just about the accident, is it? It's about something else. Something you don't want to talk about. Or some emotion you've got going that you don't like. Maybe you do feel responsible for what happened just now but it wasn't your fault.' Her dark eyes bit deep into him. 'Or something that happened in the past? God knows what because every time we stray anywhere close to deep you back off. You won't talk about your family or why you don't spend time with them, so I'm guessing it's something about that. But hey, who knows? Because I certainly don't.'

She was dangerously close to the mark and she was right too, he didn't want to talk about it.

'It's too…' He chugged out a deep breath that felt as if all his stress and anger and self-loathing filled it. How could he explain what had happened? How could he tell her the magnitude of his mistake? *Neglect.* Not mistake. 'It's history I don't want to talk about. Ground that doesn't need raking over. Stuff you don't need to know for the ball.'

'I might not need to know, but I want to know. That's what friends are for, right? We share stuff. The good, the bad and the messy.' She glared at him. A few moments ago her eyes had been shining with pride and excitement and light and he'd snuffed it out. 'Because we are friends, Lucas. Above all else. When this deal's finished, that's what we'll be.'

He didn't even want to think about what they'd mean to each other…after.

He looked at his knees. His feet. The sand. But none of them had any answers. He raised his head to look at her, struggling for words to describe what had happened. 'I don't know what to tell you, Ivy. I can't… I don't… I mean, I want to. I just…don't know how.'

She held his gaze, long and steady as if assessing him…no, *scrutinising* him. As if she had X-ray vision deep into his soul and wasn't overly impressed by what she saw there.

She had no idea.

'You want to. That's a start. I guess.' She sat for a moment, legs pulled up, arms wrapped around her knees as she stared out to sea, as if the endless ocean had the answer.

He waited. Words he couldn't say tripped through his head.

Third-degree burns. Intensive care. Poor prognosis.

Then images of his little sister, screaming in pain. Hooked up to tubes. Drugged and still, so still he'd thought she'd died. Thought he'd killed her.

Felt the shame fill every cell of his body.

How could he convey all that to Ivy and hope she wouldn't think less of him?

Eventually she said, 'So, you're not going to say you want to stop, but you're asking me to say it. Unlucky, Lucas. Because if you're leaving the decision to me then I opt to carry on. I promised I'd be your date to the ball to get your mother off your back and I will.'

Relief shimmered through him and his heart recovered. 'I don't deserve that. But thank you.'

She turned to look at him, her features softening with a small smile. 'Did we just have our first argument?'

'I think so.'

'You *think* so because I did a lot of growling and pushing, but you didn't say much at all.

That's not how arguments work.' She shivered and pulled the towel round her shoulders.

'I haven't had much experience with relationship disagreements, to be fair. But I can't say I enjoyed that one.'

'I was in a five-year thing with Grant and let's just say we perfected the art of fighting. But just a heads up, Lucas, next time it will work better if you join in and say a few things. Extrapolate a little. Tell me what's going on in your head. There's nothing worse than arguing all on your own.'

He was pretty sure she wouldn't want to know what was going on in his head. Confusion. Remorse. Attraction. Need. 'I'll try to be a better sparring partner, then.'

'Excellent.' She leaned forward and touched her lips to his, so close he could see the little rivulets of sea water dripping down her face, taste the salt. 'It's a good job I'm just in it for the sex, because you really need to work on your interpersonal skills.'

'Yeah. Thank God for that. And noted. I've got some homework to do.'

'Or your mother's going to see that we're off kilter on the communication front.'

'Practice makes perfect, then.' He grinned and kissed her again.

'Come here.' She opened her arms. 'Let's start practising our non-verbal skills too.'

He held her tight against him, pretending it was to keep her warm, or for reconciliation, but it was more than that. This hug was for him. To hold onto something good when his head was swimming with memories of that day, all those years ago when he'd been unable to protect his sister. To hold onto Ivy just a little bit longer.

Truth was, he was wildly relieved she'd said she wanted to continue their charade, deeply ashamed he didn't have words to explain to her what had happened in the past and what held him back from being the person she wanted him to be.

And scared as hell about what it all might mean.

CHAPTER TWELVE

'WE'RE KIND OF falling into a routine, I suppose. What is it they call it when you're scared of spiders, so they stick you in a room full of them? Flooding therapy? We're learning as much about each other as we can.' Ivy stepped out from the changing room in the champagne-coloured dress that Ali had picked out for her. 'Too short?'

'It's more belt than dress. You've got great legs, but I don't think it's suitable for a charity ball or meeting parents. Put it this way, they'd get to meet a lot more of you than you might want.' Harper grinned over at Ivy from her seat between Phoebe and Ali, on the velvet couch in the ball-gown shop. The third ball-gown shop they'd visited, and so far Ivy had managed to dodge the Lucas questions, but now she just couldn't as Harper pinned her with a laser look and asked, 'So this flooding therapy involves sleepovers?'

'Maybe.' Ivy feigned lack of interest. But couldn't help herself. Because if she didn't tell someone she'd likely explode with all the excitement. 'Oh, okay. He's been over four out of seven nights.'

'Wow.' Ali's eyes grew wide. 'Intense.'

Intense indeed. And wildly sexy. 'And I may have stayed over two out of seven nights at his.'

'So you're practically living together.' Phoebe looked at the other two girls and bugged her eyes. 'Are you sure that's wise?'

Ivy turned away from her friends to, ostensibly, look in the mirror at the dress…but more, to not have to look them in the eye, or for them not to see the emotions she knew would be showing on her face. Because she was so confused now about how she felt. 'It's only for another week. Then we're done.'

We can stop this any time. I won't hold you to it.

She didn't want to stop. And even though the sex was great and the connection was still tight, she felt him retreating already. Oh, he hadn't been as outspoken about it as he had at the beach, and hadn't suggested again that they stop before the ball, but he still veered away from any deep conversations about the past or relationships and shuddered every time she mentioned Harper and Yarran's engagement.

He had her back, of course. She knew he did. Unlike with Grant, she knew Lucas was as good as his word. He did what he said he was going to do. He turned up on time. He made no grand gestures or rash promises. This was fun. This was sex. This was a ruse for his parents. This was simple.

Only, somewhere along the line it had become serious too. Serious for her at least. She'd started to think that she might not be able to let him go quite so easily after the ball and she knew now, without a shadow of a doubt, that she was in far deeper than she'd planned. She liked him. Too much. Wanted him. Too much. And knew her heart was at risk again. But she couldn't put a stop to it no matter how much at risk she was.

'How about the burgundy one there?' Phoebe pointed to another rack in the corner of the room. 'Third one along with the beads on the bodice.'

'This one?' Ivy refocused on the matter in hand: a suitable dress for parent-meeting. She pulled out a slinky red number and held it up, grimacing. 'Too tight. I won't be able to eat anything.'

'No. Not the red one. The burgundy one.' Phoebe pointed to the rack then sighed and stood up. 'Let me show…oh.' She blinked. Wobbled. Put her hand out.

Ivy dashed over and put her arm out for Phoebe to steady herself. 'You okay, Phoebs?'

Her friend nodded, all the colour leeching from her face. 'I think I stood up too quickly.'

'Too much champagne at lunch? Wait…you didn't have any.' Ivy frowned. This was very unlike Phoebe, who was normally healthier than all of them. 'Not enough champagne, clearly.'

Phoebe's cheeks gained some colour. And a little bit more. 'Like I said, I'm just getting over some stupid stomach bug. I can't even think about drinking at the moment.'

Ali eyed her suspiciously. 'Are you sure you're okay? Should we take your blood pressure?'

'Honestly, that's the problem with doctor friends. Always too eager to intervene.' Phoebe laughed ruefully and slotted herself back onto the sofa. 'I'm fine. I feel much better already.'

'Did you have breakfast?'

'Are you pregnant?' A scuttle of laughter and a chorus of giggles. *As if!*

'I'd need a man for that, right?' Phoebe joked, but Ivy couldn't help noting that the joke seemed forced.

As Ivy tried on the burgundy dress she could hear Ali and Harper giving Phoebe the full interrogation on her diet and exercise regime and a lecture on the causes of a sudden drop in blood pressure, as if Phoebe wouldn't know that. But Ivy was glad someone else was in the spotlight for a change.

She tugged up the zip at the back and remembered how Lucas had slid his hands underneath her wetsuit when she'd asked him for zip help. Her body prickled at the memory. The way he made her feel with his touch and his kisses was beyond wonderful.

She smoothed down the skirt, looked in the mirror and sighed. *Oh, yes.* Phoebe had been right. This was the one. The off-the-shoulder lace bodice was studded with pearl beads and layers of organza cascaded in gentle waves from her waist to the floor. It was grown up and sophisticated with the perfect twirl factor for when she danced. It was demure yet sexy. She felt like a princess.

An older than usual princess, but one nevertheless.

She stepped back into the shop and all three of her friends stopped talking and stared at her.

Her heart hammered. 'What do you think?'

Phoebe, looking almost back to normal but still a little peaky, clapped. 'Oh, Ivy. It's absolutely perfect!'

Harper and Ali nodded in agreement and high-fived each other. 'Yay. You look fabulous.'

Ivy twirled in front of the large gilt-edged mirror. 'I hope Lucas likes it.'

'He'll love it.' Harper smiled. 'How can he not? You look amazing.'

'I feel amazing,' she had to admit. It *was* absolutely perfect.

But, with the ball and, inevitably, *the end* hurtling towards her, she didn't think she'd feel this great for long.

* * *

'We don't often get lip injuries this severe, so I'm glad you had the chance to see it first hand,' Lucas said to Chao, his new registrar. Their Thursday lunchtime ward round had been derailed with the arrival of a patient in ER requiring emergency surgery, which meant he'd have to catch up on Emma's progress later. She was on the road to recovery now and he just wanted to make sure she got over the line before those babies arrived. 'It's imperative we try to keep the cupid arch symmetry and also be very careful to rebuild the mucocutaneous junction so we don't have shifting between red and white lip.'

'Tricky.' Chao nodded, his keen interest visible only from his eyes. The rest of his face was covered by a surgical mask and cap. 'It was a nasty dog bite.'

'Indeed. Here's a life lesson: some people like to kiss their dogs. But some dogs don't like people's faces so close. I've just about finished the nasolabial flap, how about you close up the skin layer now?' Lucas stepped aside to allow Chao better access, and glanced over towards the theatre door.

His heart danced before his brain even registered that there was someone outside.

Was that Ivy he could see through the glass? Or was it wishful thinking?

He could only see the back of her, but he'd

know her anywhere. Know that hair, that stance. Yes, it was Ivy talking to her anaesthetist. She was probably scheduled for this theatre after him.

As if she could sense him, she turned round. Their eyes met. She smiled briefly then turned away to continue her conversation.

Somehow it felt as if it wasn't enough. Hell, they'd spent the last few nights together. Having the best sex of his life. How could one glance, one smile not be enough?

'Lucas?' The male voice at his side brought him back to the now.

He shifted his focus back to the very capable Chao. Lucas assessed the wound closure. 'Done? Excellent work. Really excellent. Thanks, everyone, patient is now ready to go through to Recovery, whenever our anaesthetist is ready. Chao, make sure we keep a very close eye on infection control. IV antibiotics, please. I'll go out and let Mrs Jameson's husband know that everything went well.' Via a very quick detour.

He found Ivy in Theatre Reception, chatting to someone who looked a lot like a concerned relative. He waited until she'd finished then caught her arm. 'Got a minute?'

She glanced around them. 'Just the one, I've got surgery.'

'It occurred to me we haven't made any arrangements about the ball. Getting there et cetera.'

'We could talk tonight?'

'I'm on call, remember? And I already have patients waiting in ER. It's going to be busy.'

She pulled a sad face. 'Oh, yes. And I'm on call tomorrow. Judging how it was last time with us being so short-staffed, I don't think I'll get much chance to sleep, let alone chat.'

No getting together, then. Their last time could already have been and gone. His gut tightened like a vice. 'Sometimes schedules suck.'

'I know. But we're doctors, it's just how it is.' She laid her palm on his arm. 'I'm so sorry, but I have to work for most of this weekend too. I've been trying to get out of it, but one of the general surgeons has had to dash back to Melbourne because his father's just died, and the other is away on holiday. I've at least got Samreen covering Saturday night and Sunday morning, so I'll get a chance to recover from the ball before coming back to work.'

He understood, of course he did, but his chest felt hollow. Time was running out. 'Sure. No worries. I'll come and collect you on Saturday whenever you need me to.'

'That's sweet, but I'm guessing you need to be there to support the family. Won't they need you for the set-up?'

'Probably. But they can do without me for an hour. They certainly do without me for a lot longer than that usually.'

'Not looking forward to it?'

'Now it's actually staring me in the face? No. I hate getting dressed up in a suit, might as well be a straitjacket.' He was beyond grateful he'd have her on his arm as a distraction from all his many failings that he would no doubt be reminded of. 'I can bring you straight to the hotel after work. I'll take your stuff over earlier and we can get ready together in our suite.'

Her eyes twinkled. 'Our suite? Not our room?'

'I booked one at the hotel where the ball is going to be held. That way we don't have to panic about getting home afterwards. All we need to do is walk upstairs.'

Her eyes narrowed and she looked uncertain. 'You want me to stay that night? After the ball?'

He hadn't even thought about that when he'd booked. 'I…well…'

But she laughed. 'Hey, you booked a suite. I am so going to take advantage of that. A suite! So fancy. But then, I keep forgetting that you are a Matthews.'

'I get the feeling you won't forget after Saturday.'

She stroked his arm. 'It will be fine.'

He doubted that it would be fine at all.

And this time he wasn't thinking about spending the evening with his family, but about trying to move on from Ivy the day after.

CHAPTER THIRTEEN

SO THIS WAS IT.

The end.

Although it was still only the beginning of the evening.

Ivy's heart crumpled a little as she walked across the ornately decorated five-star-hotel foyer on the arm of the most handsome man there. All dressed up in black tie, he looked like something from a movie red-carpet affair.

She felt his steadiness as they walked, the comfort of his arm. The rightness of them being together. The way it felt so natural and in step. They'd come a long way in just over three weeks from frosty beginnings to an understanding and connection deeper than anything she'd known before.

Her heart crumpled a little more, although the prospect of trying to convince everyone she and Lucas were an item kept it buoyant and agitated.

The foyer was filled with guests dressed in finery, chatting and laughing. There was a string quartet playing classical music, something she recognised—Albinoni's Adagio in G—so soulful and stirring it always made her cry. Great choice of music to sink her mood lower.

Pull on your big panties, girlfriend.

She was supposed to be happy and in love.

Love?

She looked up at the man next to her and her heart twinged. Her body automatically leaned towards him as if pulled there by an invisible thread. She liked him, yes. But love? That was a stretch. Surely?

A lump bloomed in her throat. She swallowed it away. This was supposed to be a fun evening. She didn't want to bring the vibe down. He was showing her off. They were happy. Besotted. Excited to meet his family.

Across the room she eyed some of the Sydney Central hospital bigwigs, the CEO and CFO, a couple of senior doctors and their partners. Grant standing alone in a corner, an empty glass in his hand. Looking a little lost. His eyes lit up when he glanced in her direction.

What the…? She stared at him, and he stared back, mouth agape as his gaze roamed over her.

Lucas squeezed her arm, leaning closer and whispering, 'I see him. I see the effect you're having on him in that dress, and I don't blame him, to be honest. I can't wait to strip it off you later and kiss every inch of your body. You're the most beautiful woman in this whole room. Milk it, Ivy.'

But she didn't feel like milking it. She only wanted to bask in Lucas's gaze. To have this dress stripped from her. To have him make love to her, slowly, quickly. She'd almost forgotten that her prize in this was to make Grant jealous.

Before she could say anything, she felt herself being propelled towards Grant.

Her ex's mouth went slack. 'Ivy. Wow. Hello.'

'Grant.' She nodded at him, wondering how she'd ever found him attractive. He was shorter and thinner than Lucas. His eyes not nearly so beautiful. He was just…unimpressive. 'I wasn't expecting to see you here.'

'I'm a plus one with Miriam over there.' He pointed to a tall blonde woman at the coat desk.

Ivy followed his gaze. 'Oh? Doesn't she work in the hospital pharmacy?'

'She does. But we're not together, together. Ivy, I…' He nodded and glanced up at Lucas, who was standing stock-still by her side, saying nothing. Grant swallowed. Closed his mouth against whatever it was he'd been going to say.

'Are you going to introduce us, darling?' Lucas's arm slid around her waist and suddenly she felt the sting of tears. He was playing the devoted boyfriend role so well, she almost believed it herself. But she wasn't as good at acting or pretending, she'd discovered.

She recovered herself and knew full well that Grant and Lucas must already know each other but this was a game, a power play that Lucas was determined to win. 'Oh, Lucas. This is Grant. Grant this is my…um…boyfriend. Lucas Matthews.'

There was an awkward silence while the men nodded and glared at each other like two male lions prowling and protecting their pride, ready to attack. Then Lucas pressed a kiss to her cheek. 'We'd better get going, darling. Places to be. People to see.'

As they walked away Lucas grinned like the cat who'd got the cream. 'How did I do?'

Darling.

So much of her wished that he meant it. 'What do you mean?'

'Was I possessive enough? Do you think he got the message?'

She glanced back at Grant, who was still watching her. 'I'm sure he did. It's not important now anyway.'

Lucas looked confused. 'But I thought you wanted to show him what he's missing.'

She sighed. 'I don't care about that any more. Or about him. I most certainly didn't want to encourage a conversation, or jealousy or anything.'

'Hey, wait.' He tilted her chin so she could see his eyes. 'This was the whole point of the deal for you. Are you okay?'

'I'm fine.' She shook her jaw out of his hold. This public display of affection or possession, or whatever it was, was just a little over the top even for a supposedly loved-up new couple who were apparently besotted. And then somewhere down the track but very soon…not besotted and broken up. She decided to change tack. 'Are your parents here?'

'Ah. You're nervous about meeting them. I get it. It's okay.' He wrapped her in a hug and kissed the top of her head. 'I guess the sooner we get it over with, the better.' He raised his eyebrows and nodded, took a deep breath then gestured to a group of people in the middle of the room. 'My mother is the one in the long blue gown. Dad is on the left of her. Bald.'

Even though she was at the very pinnacle of her career and reputation, Estelle Matthews seemed softer than Ivy had imagined her. Less severe than Lucas had painted her. She looked over warmly at her son and smiled. His father, Bob, was shaking the hand of another older man, laughing. But friendly, not garrulous or obnoxious or loud. 'Oh, Lucas, they look nice.'

'Looks can be deceiving,' Lucas side-mouthed.

'Don't we know it.' She squeezed his arm as his mother waved to them, beckoning them over. 'I hope we can pull this off.'

'If you don't know the answer to anything, just be vague. Ready?'

'To lie to your parents' faces? No. But let's do it anyway.' She grabbed his hand, hoping it would make them look more like a couple. Knowing that holding onto him would make her feel better about all of this.

Her heart was drumming like a percussionist on steroids. What if she messed this up? What if Mrs Matthews saw right through them?

She held her breath as the introductions were made, smiled politely at Lucas's parents, then his brothers. Each of them smiled and nodded and shook her hand. Lucas's mother even kissed her cheek. More air-kissed, to be honest.

And they were just about to embark on what Ivy knew was going to be an excruciating conversation when they were all ushered into the ballroom and taken to their seats.

'Saved by the bell,' she whispered to Lucas as he held her chair out for her.

'Only a temporary reprieve, I'm afraid.' He smiled grimly. 'You're doing great. Just be you.'

Oh, sure. Question was, who the hell was Ivy Hurst now?

A lying unscrupulous woman? A dedicated doctor? A perfect partner for their son?

She closed her eyes briefly as she realised she was all of them. At least...when they were together, she felt things could be absolutely perfect if both she and Lucas could be truly honest and open with each other. If they allowed themselves to open their hearts just a little bit more.

But he didn't want to.

She was seated between Lucas and his father…boy, girl, boy, girl style. It felt surreal, as if she were an animal in the zoo being watched, and careful not to make a false move. But she needn't have worried, Bob was a total gentleman. Their light conversation was interrupted at times by the delivery of food and speeches, but they stuck mostly to her work history and career.

Estelle was listening in from Bob's other side and interjected often. 'You have plans to stay in Sydney? Not thinking of setting up a clinic across the country anywhere?'

Ivy interpreted this as *Will you either break my son's heart by leaving, or break our hearts by taking him with you?*

She smiled, hopefully reassuringly. 'I love Sydney and my job here. I have no plans to leave.'

'Oh, good. That's very good. Nice to have family close.' Estelle blew out a deep breath, as if she'd been holding it waiting for Ivy's answer. She clearly cared deeply for her son regardless of what he said.

Ivy chose not to elucidate that she chose not to have her own family close.

'You enjoy the public system?' Bob looked startled at such an admission.

'Absolutely. It's busy, of course, and the paperwork is challenging and taking over…' she grinned at his nod of understanding '…but I do get a kick out of helping people, especially those who don't have the ability to pay. I find that side of it very rewarding. The waiting lists are long, of course, and we're constantly running to keep up, but the satisfaction that you've helped someone is pretty amazing.'

'Indeed.' He nodded, tilting his head slightly the way Lucas did.

'Do you offer pro bono work at your clinic, Dr Matthews?'

'Bob, please.' He shook his head. 'We've talked about it—'

'Oh, good. It's such a fabulous and generous thing to do. You won't regret it,' she interrupted, before he could say something like, *But I decided against it.* 'The world needs more decent people like you offering to give a helping hand. When will you start? If you don't mind me asking.' She knew it was difficult to deny the ask for help. Everyone wanted to help, didn't they? 'There are so many people on the public waiting list, the system isn't serving them as well as it could. I'm sure Lucas has told you all about it…'

'It's…' Bob looked at his wife questioningly, then smiled, his arched shoulders relaxing. 'We'll add it to the agenda first thing Monday.'

'I can't wait to hear your plans. That's fantastic.' The smile she gave him wasn't fake at all.

Lucas nudged his foot against hers. She turned to him and saw his shocked expression. He gave her a sly thumbs up and mouthed, *Well done*. He'd mentioned he'd been badgering them to offer some pro bono slots at their private clinic for a while and never got past Go.

Bingo. Score another point in her favour.

They were interrupted again, this time by George, who wrapped Ivy in a huge warm embrace. 'Ivy! So good to see you again. I hope you weren't too sore after the horse riding.' He winked and beamed at her, his eyes twinkling with mischief.

Oh, she liked this cheeky friend so much and instantly relaxed. 'Well, it's been a while, so I did ache a bit the next day.'

'The horses are there for you any time.' George looked first at Ivy then Lucas. 'We don't see enough of you. Come and stay for the weekend and we'll take the boat out on the river.'

Lucas stared blankly back as if trying to think of some kind of answer that wasn't a lie. Ivy jumped straight in to cover for him, knowing how badly he felt about not being honest with his friends and family. 'We'd love to. It's so peaceful out there. We just need to get our calendars synced. Our on-calls have been clashing a bit recently and we haven't seen anywhere near enough of each other.'

'Oh, you've met darling George?' Estelle sighed, her features shining with happiness.

Ivy felt another jolt of shame that she was stringing all these lovely people along. 'Yes. He very kindly lent us his horses for the day.' At least that wasn't a lie.

Estelle stared at her son. 'Wow. This is something.'

Lucas gave his mother a warning stare and grumbled, 'Mother.'

'Oops.' George clearly understood all the subtext of the family dynamics and winked at Ivy. 'Light the touchpaper and retreat, that's me. See you soon, Ivy. Lucas, *call me*.' He made the universal phone gesture with his hand, then he was gone.

Estelle leaned across her husband and grasped Ivy's hand. 'I know, I know. I'm sorry, I shouldn't pry, but Lucas has never talked about his girlfriends before, never mind brought one to the ball. Which makes you very special.'

'Oh, I don't think so.'

'I do.' Estelle's mouth curved upwards as her eyes roamed Ivy's face. 'I can see you are. I see the way you look at each other.'

Ivy glanced at Lucas, panic rising in her gut. Was it obvious to everyone that this had gone far deeper for her than for him? Did he see her emotions on her face?

Estelle was still talking. 'And meeting George

too? He and Lucas have been tight friends for so long, George is practically family.'

'He's lovely.' Another not-lie. Unfortunately the not-lies were far outweighed by the lies. She hated herself for agreeing to this. Estelle and Bob only wanted Lucas to be happy and they would be heartbroken when he told them it was over.

They wouldn't be the only ones.

'The things they used to get up to, and the stories George tells...oh, he's so funny. He'd make a fantastic best man. Although Lucas has his brothers too. It would be a difficult choice—'

'Ivy. Let's dance.' Lucas glared again at his mother and grasped Ivy's hand. She had no choice but to stand and walk with him to the dance floor. The band was playing something fast and it was difficult to talk, but Lucas made his displeasure with his mother pretty obvious. He twirled Ivy round. 'See what I mean about prying? About the heavy pressure? George will make a great best man...what the hell?'

'She loves you.' She twirled under his arm.

'She meddles.'

'Because she wants to see you settled and happy.' Ivy put her arms around his neck and wiggled in time to the music. Letting her hands stroke his shoulders, caress his back. It felt so good to be in his arms, even if this was the last time. Even though she felt so bad about the lies, she would not regret having had these last few weeks getting to know him. It had been magical, wonderful. 'How did we do? Do you think they believed us?'

'Definitely. You were perfect. Just perfect.' The music tempo changed to something slow and he grasped her waist, pulling her close, nuzzling his nose in her hair. 'They love you. I…'

She gripped him too. Her senses on full alert. What was he about to say? 'Yes? You…you what?'

'I…' He shook his head, his expression flatlining. 'Wanted to tell you again that you look amazing. This dress is beautiful. You are beautiful, Ivy. Thank you, for everything.'

I wish it weren't a lie. I wish it weren't the end.

Her throat filled with what felt like the pressure of unshed tears.

'Ivy…'

Her heart hammered hard as hope filled her chest. 'Yes?'

He looked down, tilted his mouth to hers and it felt as if the whole world started to ebb away. How she ached for his kisses. Even if this kept going for one night, one week, one year, she'd never have enough.

But then he stopped moving. Just stared down at her.

'What's the matter?' Her gut tightened like a vice. This wasn't a face filled with faux adoration, it was filled with panic.

This was it. This was the end. Right here. On the dance floor. And she'd still have to keep up the pretence of being happy because she would not be humiliated in front of all these people. His family. People she worked with. She would just have to keep smiling until she could break down somewhere private.

'Nothing. I mean…' He stepped away, his face pale. Eyes haunted and dark. 'I have to… I'll just be a minute.'

'But…'

He turned and stalked across the dance floor.

She frowned, watching his taut back disappear through the crowds. What was going on?

She watched him go. Probably not for the last time. They had to say a proper goodbye, at least. Surely?

But her heart followed him out of the door.

Lucas couldn't breathe.

He felt as if his chest was constricting. God, how stupid was he?

He'd almost said…done…

He'd been on the verge of kissing her, looked down and saw the expression on her face…something serene and beautiful, and the way she was looking at him, the way his mother had described, as if Ivy truly, honestly cared for him. Which he…couldn't compute. She was in this to get back at Grant.

But maybe, what if...what if she'd become embroiled in this as he had?

His heart tied itself in knots. Because, despite everything, he was glad she looked that way. He *wanted* her to look that way at him. And he'd almost...almost blurted out his feelings for her. Which, he now knew, were deep and tangled and too much.

This was *fake*. For God's sake. It wasn't real.

But the kisses were real. The lovemaking was. The heart song when he was with her was very real. The ache to be with her was too. So, yeah, his feelings for her were tangible and irrefutable, that much was clear, and he could not let them get any deeper.

With shaking hands, he untied his bow tie and tugged his shirt collar open, let the cool night air sluice the stress from his skin. Out here on the balcony he could see the city lights, heard the loud cawing of birds settling down for the night. He imagined he could see his apartment block, wished he were there with her in his arms, wound back a few weeks so he could live it all again. Wishing he could rewind his whole damned life back to that day when everything changed. So that he could pay attention, be present, be the caring brother. And then maybe he could have had a different life with Ivy. One with a future. One that he deserved.

Not like the one he was currently living where

he reminded himself every single day that he deserved nothing.

At what point had things between him and Ivy become serious and entangled? At what point had this turned from fake to real for him? He didn't know. After that first night? The horse riding? Working together? Sharing the hours of tenderness and passion?

Hell, he'd lost track of the time they'd spent together, exploring each other's bodies and minds. Somehow she'd become a part of him—the corner of his heart that was Ivy shaped had grown and now filled the space.

He sucked in more air. This was not good. He needed to minimise that space and clear his heart. He needed to play the game for a few more hours then leave. As they'd planned. Put an end to everything, before either of them got hurt. Lock away the memories of the caring, the lovemaking. The laughter. Her wide-open heart. The way she'd blown his open too. The love.

He closed his eyes as his gut snarled up.

Love?

He'd almost said it. It had come from nowhere, just an overwhelming feeling with her in his arms, the smile on her face, the music. Everything. The not wanting it to stop. The ache to whisk her upstairs.

He… Did he…?

No.

No.

He'd vowed he'd never get involved with anyone.

He forced himself to look out at the city and beyond. Westwards to the Blue Mountains. Reminded himself of the pain he'd caused before.

And that reinserted the rod of steel into his spine. He could not be responsible for anyone else. He could not love anyone while Flora was so…damaged. And, dammit, he was a reconstructive surgeon, he knew she would live with those scars for life. His life was hers. Not anyone else's.

He swallowed. He was not in love with Ivy, it was just an overreaction to the encroaching end. An overreaction to spending so much time with someone and opening his heart—as far as he was able, or allowed himself to do—to someone he knew would hold it.

But he was okay. He could do this. Yes.

He could do this.

Having regained his composure, he turned to go back and spend the last few hours with her. Then he stopped in his tracks. He could see through the glass door that she was making her way over to a table, towards Flora.

Flora? His chest tightened again. What was she doing here? Why had his sister come to this event? She never came, refused to socialise past her small, tight group of trusted friends.

Oh, hell.

He closed his eyes.

It was too late now anyway.

There was no need for him to call anything off or worry about Ivy becoming too involved here now. After talking to Flora, she'd hate him.

Almost as much as he hated himself.

Ivy wandered over and sat down at a table across the room from the Matthews family, trying to regain her composure. Should she stay and wait for him to come back? Should she go up to their suite and wait? Or just go home?

She didn't know what to do.

'Hi.' A young woman was sitting across from her. Ivy had been so consumed with confusion and dismay she hadn't noticed her.

'Oh, hi. Is it okay if I sit here for a minute? My feet are killing me. I'm so not used to wearing stilettos. Clogs are more my comfort footwear of choice.'

'Sure.' The woman gestured for Ivy to move closer. As she reached out Ivy saw her arms were covered in scars. The kind of scarring you got from serious burns.

'Thanks.' Ivy tried not to stare as she hobbled over to sit next to the woman. 'I'm Ivy. Oh, and I'm a doctor and wear rubber clogs for surgery, just in case you were wondering about my questionable fashion sense.'

'Hey, I loved clogs back in the day with all those little charms you could attach to them.' The woman laughed. As Ivy looked closer she noticed burn contracture scarring on the left-hand side of the woman's face and neck too. 'And I know who you are, Dr Ivy Hurst.'

'Oh?' Had the gossip machine whirled into action already? Was this someone else she was going to have to lie to? 'You do?'

'Lucas is my brother and I have to admit I've been snooping around, watching you two dance together. I'm Flora.' Smiling shyly, she stuck out her hand. Her other hand fluttered over her neck as if she was trying to cover up her scars.

Ivy desperately wanted to ask what had happened but didn't. It wasn't her business. She shook Flora's hand. 'Nice to meet you. I didn't see you at the dinner. All of your family were on my table. Or rather, I was on theirs.'

'God, I never usually come to these things. Boring as hell and my parents like to parade us around a bit too much for my liking. And… well… I've had enough of the gawking benefactors staring at the poor burnt girl. I'm so over that.'

'I can imagine.' Ivy was fully aware of just how many eyes had been on her and Lucas this evening. Imagine how much worse that would be if you were self-conscious of your appearance too.

'But as soon as Mum told me Lucas was bringing a girlfriend I had to come and spy. Sorry. I sneaked in after the speeches and sat where I could watch but not be seen.' Flora winced in apology. 'Lucas has never brought a date to any of these things before…not one he's willingly chosen to bring anyway. The burning questions…pardon the pun…in the family were, what's she like? Who is this mystery woman he likes enough to bring to meet us all?'

Lucas had never mentioned his sister had been injured or burnt but he had hesitated when he'd spoken about her. What had he said…? *'Flora's not a doctor, though. She was...'* His whole demeanour had changed.

Had he had something to do with the injuries?

Oh, God. Maybe he had.

Things started to fall into place. Things Lucas hadn't said about his motivation to treat burns patients. Things he hadn't told her about why his work seemed so personal to him. Because it *was* personal. Ivy's insides were roiling at the omissions. She clearly didn't know Lucas as well as she'd thought she did. Or did he not trust her? They were, after all, playing a game, right?

He hadn't shared his deepest secrets. He hadn't told her fundamental truths about his family, his life. Having a sister so badly injured must have impacted hugely and heavily on them all. 'Ah. I hope I didn't disappoint.'

'Disappoint us?' Flora's expression was one of confusion. 'Far from it. I can see how much you mean to him. And if someone can make Lucas happy after everything, then I want to thank them.'

How much you mean to him?

Not enough for him to talk about the things that mattered to him. Like his sister's burnt body.

'After…everything?' Ivy asked gently.

'Everything… The accident. Hasn't he told you?'

'No. Nothing about an accident.'

Flora looked at her arms. Ran her palm across the scrunched-up skin all along her left arm. 'It was a long time ago, but he's never really got over it.'

'I… I didn't realise. I didn't know.'

'That's my brother for you. Always keeps himself to himself. But ask him, Ivy. It'll be good for him to talk about it.' Flora's gaze wandered towards a smartly dressed, very good-looking guy walking towards them with two drinks in his hands. She smiled up at him. 'Well, I'm very glad I came, actually. This evening is shaping up to be a lot more fun than I thought it would be. First time I've enjoyed going out for a very long time. And finally meeting someone who can see past the scars makes a nice change. Very nice indeed.'

Ivy smiled to herself and didn't want to rake up the past when Flora was clearly very much living in the now. Any more questions would be intrusive, but she sure as heck needed to talk to Lucas about it all.

What accident?

They'd shared so much, why had he never talked about it and how much it affected him—if Flora was to be believed? And why not believe her? She was his little sister, she probably knew him better than most.

Her skin prickled, the way it did whenever he was around. Which meant… She looked up and there he was, back from wherever it was he'd dashed to. Standing in the corner of the room, looking frozen to the spot as he stared at her sitting next to Flora.

None of this made sense.

Unless he thought Ivy might be telling his sister the truth about their deal.

Oh, Ivy. What the hell have you done? Getting involved in all of this.

It was such a mess. Everything.

Worst of all, she didn't want to lie to his family any more than she already had. They were good people. Especially when she knew she was lying to herself too. Because despite everything she'd promised, everything she'd made him agree to, she'd fallen for him. Deeply. Irrevocably.

Panic crept through her body, making her limbs tremble. This was all too much, too far. Too deep.

She had to get out of here.

CHAPTER FOURTEEN

'WHAT ARE YOU DOING?' His voice, echoing through the hotel suite, made her freeze. Hell, she'd heard him calling her name as she'd fled the banqueting hall, registered the sound of the key-card buzz, and his sharp intake of breath. She'd expected him to speak but wasn't prepared for the tremble in his tone.

She swallowed away all the emotions tumbling through her. 'I'm packing my things.'

'You're leaving? Now?' He stood in front of her, shaking his head. His tie hung loosely round his neck, the top button of his shirt had been undone. He looked, if possible, even more handsome than before.

Not that it mattered. This was done.

She looked up into those dark eyes that made her weak with desire. More, made her weak to his charm and to the effect he had on her promises. On her heart. 'That was the deal, right? After the ball, we're done? Well, it's finished. At least, for me anyway.'

Ask me to stay. Tell me your secrets.

He nodded and shoved his hands deep into his pockets. 'You met Flora.'

'I did.'

'And you talked?'

Did he think she'd been discussing this fake dating charade?

She reached for her toiletry bag on the bed, put it in the overnight bag and slammed the rigid lid closed.

'You're angry.' He seemed surprised.

Was there any point in explaining? Probably not, but she'd feel a whole lot better. And after the brutal arguments with her parents she'd learnt to always bite back her anger, particularly with Grant, and been the capitulating girlfriend. She'd hidden the dark side of herself because she'd wanted him to only see the light in her. And look where that had got her.

But a) Lucas wasn't her boyfriend, so she could say what she damned well wanted. They were breaking this up now anyway. And b) the dark was as much a part of her as anything else, he'd said so himself. What did she have to lose?

She put her hands on the suitcase lid but didn't look at him. 'Yes, I am angry, Lucas. I'm angry that you left me alone on the dance floor looking like an idiot. I'm angry that you didn't tell me about Flora's injuries and accident. I was blindsided when I met her, to be honest.'

His eyebrows rose. 'I didn't want to make a big thing of it. I didn't think you'd get to meet her.'

She whirled to face him. 'Because this is our last day and she never comes to the ball so you thought you might get away with me not meeting her? Conveniently not telling me that she had an accident that massively impacted her life. Or that apparently you blame yourself for it.'

His jaw tightened. 'Because it was my fault.'

'How would I know?' She raised her palm and waved him away. 'I know nothing about it.'

'She…didn't tell you?' His eyes grew wider. Darker.

'No, and you look somehow relieved that she didn't share your secret.'

His jaw worked as if he were grinding his teeth or subconsciously keeping his mouth clamped closed so he didn't have to talk. But then he said, 'I'm relieved she didn't have to talk about it and therefore live through it all again.'

'Well, your sister told me to ask you about it. She wants me to know what happened. So tell me, Lucas. Tell me what happened.'

His eyes blazed anger and pain. 'Why? So I can add you to the list of people who will never forgive me? So you can see what kind of person I really am?'

Despite her own anger and frustration, she put her palm on his chest, felt his raging heart under her fingertips. 'I know what kind of person you are, Lucas. You're good and kind and sexy and funny. You're an amazing man who has a lot to give. But something inside you is stopping you from giving all of you. And I think it's to do with this accident. Whatever happened to Flora is holding you back.'

He turned away and stalked to the window. Stared out into the blackness. 'She's not the person she was. Or the person she could have been. She lost so much that day and that was my fault.'

Ivy thought of the intelligent, funny, bright woman she'd just met. 'She's not as damaged as you think, and I reckon she'd hate to hear you describe her like that. She's recovering. She's healing. She's a lot better than you allow yourself to believe her to be. Tell me.'

His back tensed. 'No.'

'Tell me, or I walk out of here right now.'

He turned slowly and glared at her. 'You should probably do that anyway.'

'For God's sake, Lucas. I am so tired of you hedging. Be honest with me. Please.' She knew her voice was getting louder and more desperate, but she couldn't help it. 'One last time. Let. Me. In.'

He looked at her for a long time and so many emotions scudded across his face. Fear. Panic. Hurt. Then he sighed and turned back to the window, his shoulders sloped forward in defeat. 'She was so little. Just turned three. I was sixteen and old enough to know better. Do better.'

'You were also just a kid, really,' she whispered, afraid that saying too much might make him clam up again.

'We were doing this stupid wilderness glamping thing in the outback in the Blue Mountains…back before glamping was a real thing. The whole family getting back to nature and all that, swag tents, bush walks, campfires. Not something we'd ever done before and it was a real adventure.

'The first morning we were due to go off on a nature walk, but Mum had to stay at the camp because Flora was too little and still asleep, and she'd had a difficult night so we didn't know when she'd wake up.'

His hands fisted into balls at his side. 'But I could see that Mum really wanted to go. So, I told her I'd stay behind and look after Flora. Truth was, I didn't feel too great because of some virus I'd caught, but I hadn't wanted to mention it in case they called the trip off. We were all so excited to be going, I didn't want to ruin everyone's holiday.'

He inhaled and then let out the breath slowly. 'So…off they went. It was early morning. The guide had cooked breakfast on a roaring campfire… I was still feeling off and hadn't had a great sleep myself, plagued by stomach pains and nausea. I was sitting in a sunny spot, reading a book and waiting for Flora to wake up.' He shook his head and turned to look at her, his beautiful face filled with anguish. 'I must have fallen asleep again. Because next thing, I was jolted awake by my little sister screaming.'

'Oh, Lucas.' Ivy could guess what had happened.

'She'd fallen into the campfire embers.'

Her hand hit her mouth as horrible images filled her head. 'It wasn't put out? Surely it's basic campfire rules?'

'The guide swore he'd put it out, but…whatever. By the time I got to her she'd got burns on her arms and legs and face. Her beautiful unblemished skin was…' He turned away. He didn't need to say anything more, Ivy had seen it. She was a doctor. She knew.

She also knew about guilt and shame and the pain when the people you love see you as less, as other, as separate. Ivy walked to him and put her palm gently on his shoulder. 'That's a lot to carry, Lucas. Too much.'

She could see his reflection in the darkened window, the pain etched on his face, held in every inch of his taut body. He shook his head. 'I should have stayed awake. It was my job. It was my duty.'

She sucked in a deep breath to try to shift the lump in her throat and the heaviness in her heart.

He'd been barely a man and an ill one at that. She knew how hard the pull of sleep was when you were sick and exhausted. 'I know a lot about duty, Lucas. And I know how deep that goes. I understand why you feel like it was your fault.'

'Because it was,' he said through gritted teeth.

'No. The guide should have made sure the fire was out. Your parents should have too. They should have seen you weren't well. Flora doesn't blame you, I'm sure of it.'

'She just doesn't say it out loud. Not like the rest of the family.'

'I didn't hear them say a single thing.'

'Not any more. But they don't have to say the words for me to hear them. Feel them in here.' He tapped his chest, and turned back to look at her, his expression crestfallen. Bereft.

She closed her eyes to stop the tears. He'd carried this with him every day. No wonder he'd chosen to be a reconstructive specialist, because if he couldn't help his sister, he could relieve some of his burden by helping others like her. But the guilt had also stopped him from giving himself, from sharing his life with other people. He'd felt he'd been responsible for Flora's life and he'd failed.

Back that day when they were horse riding he'd said he couldn't deal with Ivy getting into trouble too. She'd thought he'd meant that he didn't have enough physical capacity to save her as well as Sione. Not that he didn't have enough emotional space. Then again when kite surfing he'd said he was responsible for her little head knock. Even though he wasn't. He took safety very seriously and here was the reason. The desperately sad reason.

'You have to move on from this, Lucas. Flora has. It's clear she doesn't think you're to blame.'

'I don't need her forgiveness when I can't forgive myself.' He turned back to the window and stared out for a long time. So long she felt the moment had passed for them to continue the conversation. He was clearly taking time to gather himself. To grieve. To…what else she didn't know.

She didn't want to leave him here in this fug, but she also didn't know what to do. This deal was over. Their 'relationship' was over. That had been the plan. And he hadn't given her any indication of wanting otherwise.

So, quietly she zipped up her overnight bag and slipped her trainers on. Picked up her phone and started to search for the taxi number.

He turned to look at her. 'What are you doing?'

'Calling a taxi.'

'No.' He took two steps towards her, his face filled with sadness and pain and need. So much need. For company, she imagined. For affection, for a balm and distraction. He reached a hand out to her. 'Stay, Ivy. Stay, please.'

Stay. It was all she'd wanted to hear from him these last few days. The want in his voice had her dropping the phone onto the bed. She wouldn't ask what he meant by that. Whether he meant all night. All week or for ever.

But she took his face in her hands and kissed him. Tried to kiss away the pain and the guilt and the torture of having seen his little sister go through so much, and to feel responsible. Kissed away the shame. Kissed away the hurt.

And kissed into him everything she knew him to be now. A good man, a devoted surgeon, a compassionate doctor who must have repaid his debt over and over with his dedication and his skills. A wonderful, thoughtful, sexy man.

As she kissed him she felt his body respond. His kisses became urgent, his hardness pressed against her centre. She was lost in his taste once again. His gaze was tender and soft and there was something almost ethereal about his touch. Like an echo or a shadow tracing over her skin.

He wanted her, she knew, as much as she wanted him, but he couldn't allow himself to fall into more than what they had now…sex, fun times. Nothing serious. No commitment. He was too damaged. Too filled with shame and hurt to let other emotions in. Too locked up inside the memory and guilt to allow himself to break free.

But when he turned her around and slowly

unzipped her beautiful dress she closed her eyes and let the need overwhelm her too.

When he kissed the nape of her neck she pressed against him, when he slid deep inside her she held him tight. Hoping it could last for ever, but knowing that some dreams were impossible.

After, he held her close and she watched him drift to sleep. Settled again. But for how long?

They could be a perfect match. But…he couldn't do it. She'd seen it in his eyes. Felt it in his kisses. As if he was letting her go, kiss by kiss. Touch by touch.

He was letting her go.

And she would leave, because that had been the plan. No amount of wanting could change that. No amount of loving him could make him love himself, and then allow himself to love her too.

Her throat felt raw and thick, her chest heavy with grief. She forced her eyes closed, would not allow herself to cry again over a man. She was done with that.

She'd come into this for a stupid deal around her own insecurities, trying to win some petty game against a man she didn't even care for, and hadn't counted on falling for Lucas. Hadn't contemplated losing her heart to someone who didn't have the capacity to fall for her.

I love you.

There it was.

She loved him.

No matter how much she'd tried not to. No matter how many lies she'd told herself: that this was fake, this was temporary, there was no time to learn to love him, faults and all. That she was in control.

Because she wasn't. She did love him. Wholly, totally. Irrevocably.

And now she would be forced to see him at work, bump into him in the corridors, on the wards. Hear his laughter, his voice. Watch his tenderness in action, with his patients and colleagues.

She would be forced to stand on the sidelines of his life with just the memories of this precious time when she'd been caught up in the magic of Lucas Matthews.

As quietly as possible she slipped from his arms, then the bed, careful not to wake him. She dressed and booked a taxi to take her home. Her body alive with the imprint of his touch, and her heart breaking.

She pressed a soft kiss to his forehead, careful again not to wake him up. After years of carrying guilt and shame he deserved some peace.

I love you.

Wishing this could last a lifetime.

But knowing it was their last goodbye.

CHAPTER FIFTEEN

I love you. Had she said that? Had he imagined it? A dream, maybe?

Lucas lay in the comfort of the hotel bed, eyes still closed, in that foggy space between sleep and wakefulness and his heart…swelled. He'd told her everything. The world hadn't fallen in. In fact, the space in his heart that was Ivy-shaped had grown even bigger.

What would it be like to have this all the time? This connection and warmth in his chest? This feeling that he wasn't alone, that someone was looking out for him. Her…love.

His heart juddered. Had she said that? Her voice had been so quiet he wasn't sure.

She loved him?

Geez, he didn't know what to think or feel other than a good deal of panic, a smattering of hope. So many things. Did he love her?

Again. The same answer as last night. He cared for her, but love? That whole for ever thing?

Pointless analysing it. He didn't know if he

could love anyone. But if he could, Ivy would be top of the list. The only one on the list.

After the heart-searching on the hotel balcony he'd come to tell her it was over, but when he'd seen her packing he'd panicked, realising his head and his heart were acutely at odds. Too much had been swirling round his mind. He'd wanted her so badly, and yet understood that making more of this would be a mistake.

But she'd stayed. That was something.

He reached to her side of the bed to pull her close. Her side, yes. Because they'd fallen into a delightful routine. A life. Together.

She wasn't here.

He jolted upright and peered at the empty bed and then scanned across the room.

No beautiful dress slung over the sofa where he'd thrown it last night after reverently removing it from her perfect body. No glittery sandals. Her bag was gone.

He jumped out of bed, his chest contracting like a vice around his heart. There was no sign of her in the bathroom. He ran back to the bedroom and ran his hands over the sheets. Her side of the bed was cold.

She'd been gone some time.

She'd left him.

Ivy. He slumped onto the mattress, holding his head in his hands. She'd gone. As he'd expected her to. As he'd wanted…before.

Where had she gone?

If she loved him, *why* had she gone? He needed to talk to her.

He grabbed his phone and quickly scrolled for her number. But as he stared at it he remembered that first night, making the deal. The idea of her getting revenge on her ex if she pretended to be his girlfriend.

And reality sank in. She'd gone because that had been the arrangement. The deal was over. Kind of like his life. Because what was his life now she wasn't in it?

Could he carry on as if this hadn't happened? As if she hadn't made a permanent mark on his heart? And where the hell did the idea of her saying *I love you* come from? Wishful thinking? Well, that was a one-eighty swerve from his no-commitment promises. He should be relieved she'd left him without any drama, without him having to make excuses or…

'Ivy!' he shouted her name. 'Ivy.' But there was no relief, just a sharp stabbing in his chest.

Eventually, after God knew how long he'd been sitting there staring at her number numb with indecision, he slunk into the shower and washed away the scent of their lovemaking, all trace of her. Gone.

He grabbed a towel and slung it round his hips. Dripped through to the lounge and sat on the sofa unsure what to do now. Unsure what was next.

Because he'd expected this to end, but hadn't expected the weight in his chest to be this heavy or the grief to be this acute.

He'd told her everything and his world had, in fact, fallen in.

Because she'd gone.

Ivy threw her overnight bag onto the bed and closed her eyes tight to stop the tears from flowing. Tears that she'd been trying not to shed since she'd left that hotel suite.

But it was getting harder and harder, the further she was away from him.

Her phone rang.

Alinta.

Not ready to talk to anyone yet, she ignored it and started to unpack. She hung her dress on the bedroom door, and stroked it. It had been wonderful to walk into the ball on his arm. And yes, to see Grant's haunted face. To meet Lucas's family. Lovely Flora, who bore him absolutely no blame. If only he could see that.

Her phone rang again.

Phoebe.

Ivy refused to pick up. Because what could she say?

I was in control. I agreed not to get involved. I promised not to fall in love. I've made the biggest mistake of my life.

It wasn't as if they didn't warn her. And there

she'd been, cocky and confident that she wouldn't lose her heart again.

A beep. A message to the four friends' chat group from Harper.

Well?? Ivy?? How did it go?

Ivy barely had any energy, and certainly little enthusiasm to go into details, but if she didn't answer the girls would be round in person and she couldn't face them. She typed out a reply.

It went.

A quick-fire response from Harper.

What do you mean?

Time for some honesty because, truly, Ivy was all out of lying to everyone.

We did what we agreed to do.

Alinta jumped straight back.

You broke up?

Ivy inhaled on a sob. Swallowed her sadness away. Tried to, at least. She would not cry. She was a fool who'd broken the deal by getting involved. She only had herself to blame.

She typed back.

How can we break something that was never something in the first place?

Harper:

Oh, hon. We'll be over ASAP.

No. Not least because she had to start her shift in a few hours.

Oh, she wanted a hug and some girl time, but not yet. She needed time and space to get her head around all this before she could face anyone else. How to refuse without sounding ungrateful or unfriendly?

But then her beeper pinged.

There was a surge of hope in her chest. Lucas? He hadn't called or messaged, or turned up here searching for her, wondering where she'd gone in the middle of the night. He clearly didn't care enough to find out, which she'd known all along.

And anyway, he'd phone or text, not use her work beeper.

Stupid woman.

Her heart was getting ahead of itself. Actually, her heart needed resuscitation or life support or something drastic to ease this ache right in the centre of her chest, of her life.

She loved him.

She hit her forehead with the palm of her hand. 'Stupid woman. Stop, stop, stupid woman. You are way too old for all of this.'

After she read the message she breathed out a little. Then typed a message to the group chat.

Sorry. Samreen needs me at work. Urgent splenectomy.

It was a relief to have something else to think about. She was doing exactly what she'd done after Grant, throwing herself into work, and quite frankly she didn't care. She loved her job. Other than her friends it was her only constant. The one thing she could rely on and she'd put it in jeopardy with her silly deal. What if it had all unravelled in front of her bosses?

Work was the only way to deal with heartbreak. Okay, getting drunk with her friends could also help her forget the man she loved.

No. Nothing would erase Lucas from her heart.

But friends might make it bearable.

Hammering at the door drew Lucas from…where had he been? He wasn't sure. It was cold in the hotel suite now and he was still sitting here in his towel staring at Ivy's name on his phone.

Was she…here?

'Ivy!' He dashed to the door and threw it open, his heart snagging in surprise. 'Oh. Flora. Hello.'

'Morning.' After giving him a quick peck on the cheek she peered first down at the towel then round him into the room. 'Oh. I hope I'm not interrupting anything, but I wondered if you and Ivy fancied a quick coffee before I head off home.'

He stood back and let her in, knowing she'd walk right in anyway, and tried not to let his gaze settle on her scars. She was a constant reminder of his failures. 'Actually, I'm just heading back to my place.'

To, probably, stare endlessly at nothing for another few hours, wishing he'd done things very differently. Story of his life.

Flora walked round in a circle then put her palms out in question. 'Um. Where is she? Shower? Bed? Oh, don't tell me… I did interrupt something.' She winced. 'God, sorry, big brother.'

He blinked, not understanding. 'Who? Ivy?'

Flora flicked her hand at him. 'Yes, of course Ivy.'

Lucas breathed out heavily. 'She's…gone.'

'Gone as in needed to get back to her apartment to feed her cat or something? Or gone as in…' She peered closer at him, scrutinising him the way only a sibling could. Then she frowned and shook her head disappointedly. 'Oh, Lucas. Not again.'

'What do you mean *again*?' He couldn't remember ever feeling this kind of hopelessness over a woman before. And also, how could his sister read him so well?

Flora huffed. 'What is it with you and women? They never seem to hang around.'

'Out of design.'

'You like being lonely?'

'I'm not lonely.' He hadn't been until he'd woken up and found Ivy gone.

'Liar. I liked Ivy. She was nice and funny and far too good for you.' Flora gently punched him on his biceps. 'Joking. But she is lovely, Lucas. You seemed to like her last night. Couldn't take your eyes off her.'

Because it hadn't been fake.

Here it was. Time for the answer he and Ivy had been rehearsing for the last few weeks and the statement he knew Flora would relay back to his parents. 'Things just didn't work out. You know how it is. Timetables never quite in sync… we thought we'd call it a day.'

'I don't believe you. Not after the way you looked last night.' She slumped down on the brocade sofa, chin in her hands. 'Oh, Lucas. What did you do?'

'Why do you assume it's because of something I did?'

'Because it's always something you did. Ivy is lovely and she clearly adores you.' She sat back and shook her head, sighing. She was quiet for a moment and then jolted forward. 'Oh, God. Lucas. Was it because of me? I told her to ask you about the accident. You told her?'

'Yes. I did.'

'And you told her it wasn't your fault, right?'

'You know it was. Look at you, Flora.' He could barely look at her without remembering that day. The moment everything changed.

She ran her hand over the scarring on her left arm then glowered at him. 'Lucas. For goodness' sake, stop it. I am so over this. You feeling sorry for yourself, blaming yourself. Smothering me with your over-protection. Refusing to move on from it. It's been over twenty years. I've moved on, you need to move on too. I'm *fine*.'

How could she be? After all that pain and the operations and physiotherapy? 'You're not—'

'Whoa!' Her nostrils flared and her eyes sparked fury as she held her palm up to shut him up. 'Don't you dare say I'm not fine, Lucas. Don't you dare diminish me. Sure, I've got scars and they're not pretty. I've accepted I'm not going to win any beauty contests, and that's okay. But I like who I am, scars and all. I'm a good person. I've got a great life, a good job and after you left last night I even met someone who actually likes me for who I am inside as well as out. It's time you started liking who you are too.'

She was actually a little scary and he was starting to feel a little vulnerable here in just a towel rather than his work-suit armour. Any clothes, really. 'That's easy for you to say, Flora.'

'You lifted me out of the fire. You called for help. You *saved* me, Lucas.'

He sat down next to her. Had he saved her? No…well yes, he'd done those things too, but he hadn't stopped her falling into it in the first place. He'd spent all his years since the accident protecting her, trying to make amends. Or, in her words, smothering her. 'You should never have fallen into it in the first place.'

'So? Bad things happen, Lucas. I was three years old and a bit of a tearaway like you used to be. Remember that? How carefree you were before the accident? Mum used to say you were the joker in the family and then you…weren't.'

He shrugged. 'People change.'

She reached over and put her palm over his hand. 'I don't blame you for what happened. I never have. So, instead, you blame yourself and refuse to be happy. Can you imagine how that makes me feel? Because of something I did all those years ago I get to watch you steep yourself in blame and hurt, and curtail your joy because you think you don't deserve to be happy again. Well, it's time to take your hair shirt off and stop punishing yourself, Lucas. Because the best way to feel better about what happened is to find happiness. *That* would make me happy. Seeing you in love and living your life would make me happy. Not this…' She waved her hand at him. 'Pushing people away, being too afraid to commit, feeling responsible. You're not responsible for anyone's life but your own. Or anyone else's happiness. So go out and damned well find some.'

She blinked rapidly then and looked almost as shocked as Lucas felt at her outburst. Flora, his timid little sister, had grown up. Not just that, she was incredible. How had he not seen that before?

Because he was too intent on whipping himself with a metaphorical stick. Seeing her as trapped as he was by the accident. But somewhere along the line she'd flown free, whereas he'd tightened the ropes around his life and kept everyone out.

Go figure. She was incredible and insightful too.

But he had a feeling there was only one thing that could make him happy and that was Ivy. 'It's too late. Ivy's gone.'

'Why? You clearly care about her. Doesn't she feel the same way about you?'

'I don't know.'

'How so?'

He couldn't confess about the deal now. Admit the whole relationship had been fake. Then messy and wonderful. And now ended. 'It's complicated.'

I love you.

Had he dreamt it?

'Okay, dial back a bit, bear of little brain.' Flora was smiling now, looking at him as if he were a small child she was very fond of. 'I'll start with easy questions. We can work up to difficult later. Firstly, do you love her?'

'Easy?' He closed his eyes as images of Ivy swam in his head. Ivy laughing. Ivy naked. Ivy... Her smile and her tenderness, her generosity of spirit. He ached for her. He missed her. So damned much. It was only and always her. He had never admitted anything like this to anyone before. Hell, he'd never felt like this before.

He raised his head and looked at his sister. Took a deep breath. 'Yes. I think I do. I love her.'

And he'd let her go. Forced her away with his intransigence.

'Whoop.' Flora clapped her hands. 'So what are you going to do?'

'What can I do? She's gone.'

'Oh. Lucas. Lucas.' A disdainful shake of her head. 'You're a brilliant surgeon and a wonderful man but hopeless at romance.'

'What can I say? I haven't had much practice.'

Sex, yes. Love…not so much. Not at all in fact. Until now.

Flora's eyes lit up. 'Well, now's your chance. You have to tell her.'

'What if she doesn't want me?'

I love you.

Had it been a dream? He didn't think so. And he'd thrown it all away by not allowing himself to love her back. Bloody fool.

Flora squeezed his hand. 'Is she worth the risk?'

'Oh, yes.' He nodded. Resolute. Panicked. Kind of scared about how she'd react. But yes, resolute. 'More than anything.'

Flora laughed. 'Well, I suggest you put some clothes on and come up with a plan.'

CHAPTER SIXTEEN

'THANKS, EVERYONE. GOOD WORK,' Ivy said to the operating theatre team as she finished closing up their patient. 'You can take him through to Recovery now.'

Recovery.

That would be nice.

Work was great at distracting her from the ache in her chest, but it didn't stop it. Was there somewhere called Recovery where you could go to heal a broken heart, not just a broken body?

It's called time.

Too bad it had been less than a week. She missed Lucas. Found herself looking out for him down every corridor, in every ward, in the cafe. But somehow their paths hadn't crossed yet. Or he was avoiding her.

She'd heard on the grapevine he'd immersed himself in helping his parents set up their pro bono clinic and that gave her a huge sense of pride. But…she hadn't seen him.

They were bound to bump into each other

eventually and she wasn't sure how she was going to react. He still hadn't messaged her, hadn't called. It was as if their affair hadn't even happened. He really was glad she'd gone. While she ached. So much. Walking away had taken every ounce of courage she'd had but it hadn't stopped her wanting him. Dreaming about him. Wishing things could have been so different. She loved him. That was all.

That was *everything.*

'You okay, boss?' Samreen asked her as they paused to write up the surgery notes.

Ivy glanced at her junior, who had become more friend now than colleague. 'I'm fine. Why?'

Samreen smiled softly. 'You've been very quiet these last few days. I mean… I know it's none of my business, but just checking you're okay.'

The same thing Alinta had said when they'd met up for a coffee and that Harper had mentioned over a glass of wine after work. It felt as if the world was tiptoeing around her. *Here's Ivy. Handle With Care*. That was what broken hearts did to you. They made you vulnerable and soft. Well, she wasn't going to be like that any more.

She snapped her gloves off decisively and threw them in the bin. 'Samreen, I'm fine. Thank you for noticing and asking. But I did a stupid thing and now I'm living with the consequences.'

Samreen's eyes grew bigger. 'You? Stupid? No way.'

'Unfortunately, yes. I met a guy and liked him more than he liked me. It ended. You know how it goes.' This was probably way too much information, but it was honest. She'd decided there had been too many lies recently and she was going to be honest from now on, or say nothing.

To be fair, she'd probably stick to the say nothing part a little more because it hurt too much to say the words *I love him and I miss him* out loud.

Samreen shrugged. 'I married my first love, so I'm afraid I don't know. But I can imagine. I'm sorry, Ivy.'

'Thanks. Well, I'm over it now.' If she said it enough it might sink in.

Samreen's eyebrows rose as if to say, *Really?* 'If you need a chat, I'm here.' Then her bleeper blared and she glanced down. 'Sorry, Ivy. Got to go.'

'See you.' Ivy inhaled deeply. Right. A quick shower and then Friday night drinks with the girls. She'd have to put on her game face. Or maybe tell them exactly how much she was still hurting. Stop pretending.

Half an hour later she stepped out of the theatre suite and stopped short, her heart hammering hard against her ribcage. Her belly did a little jig.

Déjà vu?

She closed her eyes. Opened them again. Yes, it was Lucas, looking devastating in a pale blue collared shirt and navy chinos. And his expression…so dark.

He was here for her? No. He hadn't been in contact, he wasn't here for her. He must be waiting for a patient. Just as she'd imagined, they'd bump into each other sometime.

Oh, well, here goes nothing. Big breath.

'Lucas?'

'Ivy.' He stood, so serious. He did not run to her, did not kiss her. Did not do any of the things she'd secretly hoped he would do. As they did in the romcoms.

Her heart-hammering turned into full-blown tachycardia. 'What is it? What's happened?'

He took one step towards her. 'Can we talk?'

'Here?' She gestured to the theatre block behind her. 'Really? You want to do this here?' Whatever *this* was.

'I don't care. Anywhere.' But he took her arm and walked her into the wintry sunshine and up to the hospital's lush rooftop garden. He gestured to her to sit on a bench, but she stood tall.

'What's this about, Lucas?'

'Us.'

She raised her palm. 'There is no us. You've made that abundantly clear since we started this thing.' Except, she noted, the sleepovers, the sex, the fun and games. The intense conversations. But he hadn't trusted her with his deepest secrets, or with his heart.

He shook his head. Took her hand. 'I know, and I'm sorry. I kept telling myself it was all some kind of dream…this feeling, every time I saw you. When you laughed and my chest heated. When I saw you hard at work and my gut tightened in pride. When I watched you come, all undone and satisfied. I kept trying to put a distance between us, a veil of pretence that this dream wasn't real. Couldn't be real. Because I don't deserve to have this, Ivy. I don't deserve to feel this way. To be happy.'

She made him happy and he was fighting it.

Oh, Lucas.

'Yes, you do. You just don't want to be happy. You've spent most of your life being ashamed and guilty for something that happened when you were a boy. You're scared.'

He looked at his feet, then back at her. 'I am. Yes. I'm scared about being responsible for you, protecting you. And failing.'

'I'm quite capable of being responsible for myself.' So this was just an apology. Too little too late. Her heart felt as if it were collapsing in on itself.

He gave her a hesitant smile. 'I know that now.

I wouldn't dream of being responsible for you. Maybe alongside you, though? Flora pointed out that I've been an idiot for years, trying to cut myself off from everyone as some sort of punishment.'

'An idiot, eh? I do like your sister.'

He huffed out a breath. 'Well, she's right. I'm also scared of letting all that go and just…being part of something. I've never had a relationship that lasted longer than about ten minutes, never mind a lifetime.'

'It was a fling, Lucas. No, it wasn't even a fling, it was *pretend*. Fake.' Because she didn't dare hope where this was going, she gave him an out.

But he looked as if she'd just punched him in the stomach. 'Is that how you feel? Because if that's what you really believe then I'll walk away, right now. Just say it's over and I'll go.'

Stay.

Tears pricked her eyes. She would not cry. 'Oh, Lucas. This is not how I thought things would play out. I—'

'Wait.' He held up his index finger. 'We're tying ourselves in knots here. Can I ask you a question?'

She pressed her lips together, trying not blurt out, *I love you, you idiot,* and eventually managed, 'Sure.'

'That last night, in the suite. After we'd made love. Did you tell me that you loved me?'

'What?' Had she? Had she said those words out loud as she'd left him? 'I…don't think so.'

'It must have been wishful thinking, then.' He swallowed, panic rushing across his features. 'So, you don't love me?'

'I…' God, how much of a fool was she going to make of herself now?

He took her other hand and gazed into her eyes. 'Because I love you, Ivy Hurst. I love you so much. God knows, I tried not to, but I've fallen hard. I want you. I miss you. I want to grow old with you. I want *us*. For ever.'

'Us. Yes. Us.'

He loved her? A rogue tear escaped down her cheek.

He leaned in and kissed it away. 'I'm so sorry about not being honest with you about how I feel. I promise that, if you'll have me, I'll tell you every day how much I love you.'

'I'll hold you to that.' She couldn't stop the smile growing deep inside her heart reaching her face. He'd come a long way and he wanted to keep on trying. How could she not love him? Or trust and believe in him? 'I do love you, Lucas.'

'You do?'

She nodded and squeezed his hands. 'I do.'

'Words I hope you'll repeat to me some day. With a ring.'

What was he saying? Her heart swelled. 'Whoa. Wait. What? Are you…?'

He dropped her hands and then…suddenly, he was on one knee. Somehow, he'd magicked a small velvet box into his right hand and was opening it.

Was that…? She couldn't believe it. A beautiful, glittering diamond ring. *Oh. My.*

He cleared his throat. Her strong, perfectly confident man was nervous. 'Ivy Hurst. I love you. You make my world perfect. You are perfect in every way. Would you…will you…marry me?'

This was a surprise. A pinch-me, exciting surprise. She blinked back more tears. 'You've come a very long way from a no-strings fling.'

He grinned. 'I got swept off my feet by an amazing, wonderful, beautiful woman. What can I say? Other than, will you have me? After all this? Please. Don't keep me waiting. My knee's killing me.'

She giggled. 'Yes. Yes, of course. I'll have you *because* of all this, Lucas. You've shown me how to overcome the worst things imaginable. To learn how to listen to your heart. To trust in someone. And in love.'

'You taught me all those things too. And

more.' He stood, slid his arms around her waist and drew her closer. 'Now, let's go celebrate.'

She winced. 'I'm supposed to be meeting the girls.'

'Do you think they'd mind, just this once, if I stole you away for a private celebration? It's not every day you decide to spend the rest of your life with someone.' He took her hand and walked her out of the garden and down to the car park. His little sports car was parked right there, the roof concertinaed back, the back seat filled with flowers. 'For you. Everyone knows the world is a better place with plants, right?'

'Oh, Lucas.' She gasped at this out-of-character romantic gesture from a resolute commitment-phobe. And then remembered all the romantic things he'd done already: the horse riding, the picnic, the kite surfing. He hadn't been holding back, he'd just wooed her with stealth. And she'd fallen. Utterly. 'You remembered. That first night at my place.'

'I'll never forget one moment of being with you. I love you, Ivy.'

'I love you too, Lucas.'

'Never stop saying that.' He wrapped her into his arms and kissed her again, long and deep and hard.

'Hey! You two! Congratulations!' Harper and Ali were walking towards them and cheering, waving their arms in the air.

'Woot!' Phoebe cried out. 'Get a room!'

'That's the plan! But I'm going to have to take a rain check on drinks.'

'Go for it,' Harper called as Ivy climbed into the car and waved at them. 'Call us!'

'I will!'

'We want all the details.'

'Later.' She blew them a kiss.

Then Lucas charged the engine and they drove off towards their future, with the wind in their hair and a lifetime of love in their hearts.

* * * * *